Island of Souls
LIGHT WITHIN THE DARK

a novel

Island of Souls
LIGHT WITHIN THE DARK

a novel

Milan Ljubincic

Fig Tree
C A N A D A

Figtree Publishing Group
1 Yonge Street, Suite 1801, Toronto, ON, M5E 1W7, Canada.

Learn more about the author at www.Ljubincic.com

Cover design, Ravven.
Interior book design, David Moratto.
Palmyra Atoll map courtesy of the NOAA & Wikimedia Commons.

Library and Archives Canada Cataloguing in Publication

Ljubincic, Milan, 1978-, author
Island of souls : light within the dark : a novel / Milan
Ljubincic.

Issued in print and electronic formats.
ISBN 978-0-9921311-0-4 (pbk.).--ISBN 978-0-9921311-1-1 (pdf)

I. Title.

PR9619.4.L535I85 2014   823'.92   C2014-900991-7   C2014-900992-5

Printed in Canada.
First Printing.

10 9 8 7 6 5 4 3 2 1

*For my beautiful parents Slavoljub and Luca,
my sisters Snezana and Tanya, my brother Steve,
and my global Soul family wherever you may be.
Thank you for your loving support and encouragement.*

Author's Note

From a very young age, I found myself asking some of life's greatest questions—Who am I? Why am I here? What is my meaningful contribution to this life? It led me down the path to becoming a psychologist, so I could understand humanity, the world, and our existence. But the answers didn't come quickly, and by no means easily. It was only in my early 30's that the mist had lifted and things started making sense. As my life path unfolded it became apparent to me that there exists a power far greater than each one of us; that synchronicity is real, and that every experience and encounter we have is just as it was meant to be.

The search for purpose and meaning is a very human journey. We must continuously be looking for ways to expand our knowledge, expand our conscious awareness, contribute in some sort of way, and recognize that our deeper purpose and meaning evolves over time. There may be struggles along the way, and the answers we seek will not always come when we ask for them. But they will show up eventually, and sometimes in ways we least expected, and only when we are ready to embrace their truth and teachings.

Throughout our human experience, we will feel both joy and despair in equal measure. The light exists, and so does the darkness. They each play a pivotal part in their own unique way. There will come a time when we must step into our fears to know our strengths and expand our spiritual awareness and evolution. In doing so, we must never lose sight of the light, even if the flame is small and a soft glow is all we see. When we choose to live from the *heart*, we have chosen to live in the *light*.

The interwoven psychological and spiritual insights in this allegorical tale are some of the guiding principles I have been blessed to receive, and have adopted into my own life journey. Written as a parable with a blend of metaphors, archetypical figures, sacred symbolism, and a twist of historical fiction, I now invite you to join me on a heart-warming adventure to the mysteriously enlightening Island of Souls.

Love, Light, & Blessings

Milan Ljubincic
Spring 2014

Contents

We sometimes need the darkness
to remind us of the light.

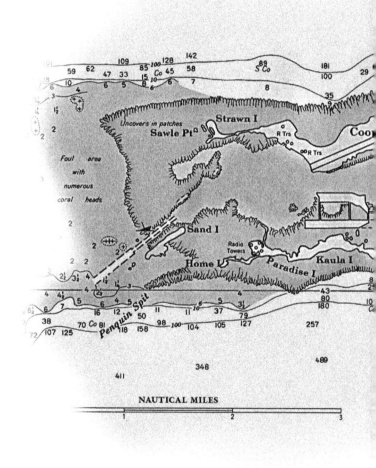

91   109   128   142
59   62   85 100 58   181
     47   33   15 10 45   89   100   29
  10   6   5   8 10 6   7   S Co
6   6   8   6   8
3   4
1½   35

Uncovers in patches
2   Strawn I
                    Sawle Pt   R Trs   Coo
2   R Trs
Foul   area
with
numerous
coral   heads
2
                                              Sand I
2   2
                         Radio
2   2   Towers
2   Home I   Paradise I   Kaula I
2¼ 3½   4   1½   8
      4   2½   4   3   43   2
4   4½   4   6   5   80   10
6   7   16   6   5   3½   180   Co
38   70 Co 81 50   11   11 10 8 37   79
72 107 125   118 158 98 100 104 105 127   257

348   489
411

NAUTICAL MILES
1   2   3

Palmyra Atoll

Mercator Projection
Scale 1:47,750

Soundings in Fathoms
At Mean Lower Low Waters

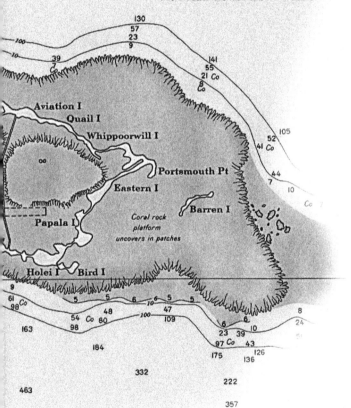

I

"I think it's about lunch time, wouldn't you say, Blue?" Blue is my Australian cattle dog. I take him with me everywhere I go.

Pulling myself up from my seat, I raise my arms and stretch. I head up top to check our coordinates and Blue follows. We have been at sea for almost 28 days, with a couple days rest in Hawaii. The ship is a 38-foot catamaran, affectionately named Betsy. According to the navigation system, Blue and I are only sixty nautical miles from our final destination, a small atoll named Palmyra. The spinnaker has caught the wind, so I drop the main sail.

Autopilot appears to be right on course, so I turn to make my way down to the galley. As I step away from the wheel, a cold chill jogs down my spine, stopping me in my tracks. The breeze is warm and the sun is shining, so the chill catches me off guard. At my feet, a faint whimper from Blue. Something has unnerved the both of us. I scratch him between the ears and scan the sea for a minute or two. Nothing's amiss. Maybe the solitude is making me jumpy. The constant quiet has put me out of sorts.

Blue and I recover from our sudden anxiety and head for the galley. I look at him and smile as he wags his tail.

As the feeling wears off, I can't help but notice how tense I'd been. Something really spooked me up there.

In the galley I put Blue's food bowl down for him and take a deep breath, trying to shake the last, lingering sense of foreboding. I reach to open the pantry, and am again overcome by a flutter of sensation. My stomach flips and tightens and my head feels as though it's about to float away from my body. If a patient described this to me, I'd say it was a panic attack, but I've never had a panic attack in my life. It's weird, almost as if my body is sending signals my mind can't understand.

I lean against the kitchen counter to gather my thoughts. I've never felt so uneasy. There's an overwhelming sense of urgency, but I can't put my finger on the reason for it. Almost as if something demands my immediate attention, but I have no idea what it is. It's like one of those nightmares where you awake drenched in sweat and panting—and you can't remember why. The kind that haunts you for a day or two. Learned behavior, I tell myself—a result of the usual nonstop schedule I maintain back home. Maybe I'm still adjusting to life at sea without back-to-back patient appointments and a laundry list of things to do. Maybe I'm just having trouble living without chaos and clutter. I take a few deep breaths and recover, again.

I open the pantry and pull out a loaf of bread, baked fresh the night before. As I turn to the small mini-fridge behind me, I feel the next surge. The fear I've been fighting takes me fully in its clutches. There is something more intense going on than vacationer's guilt. Elusive but severe, the slippery nature of this anxiety is taking its toll. The peace I've felt for the entire trip is all but gone, replaced by a sense of being on the brink of catastrophe. But how? Why?

Lunch abandoned, I turn to take a look out the port side window. My eyes scan the horizon — a blue ocean against an even bluer sky. Moments ago, my GPS showed that we were still a ways out from Palmyra, but there's something tugging at me, insisting that I investigate whatever it is that might be causing this sudden disquiet.

My eyes move restlessly across the surface of the water. Then, I see it. There appears to be a reef, or maybe even land, there in the ocean. I edge closer, my forehead touching the glass, squinting hard in the direction of what seems to be some kind of land mass. I see it clearly now, it's a coral reef!

"How strange," I say aloud. "We shouldn't be anywhere near a reef."

I run to the wheel, disengage the autopilot, and swing the helm to lee to tack away from the reef. As I turn into the wind to slow down the vessel, I see the wind indicator snap away from the masthead. As I struggle to drop the now entangled spinnaker, the wind softens and Betsy pushes gently forwards across the ocean surface. *That was too close!* I double-check my GPS; it still shows Palmyra fifty miles away. I'll have to get this looked at when I return home.

2

As I narrowly avoid disaster in the equatorial North Pacific Ocean, you may be wondering how I got to be on a yacht, sailing to an uninhabited island a thousand miles from civilization. Let me reach back in time, one year earlier, to the moment this entire story began.

This isn't the first time I needed to escape the life I know. I've been on retreats here-and-there, hiked into the wildness alone, but nothing as extreme as this. Sure I have issues, but who doesn't right? To feel emotions is to be human they say, and I know that all too well.

For me it's the dark monster within, that feeling of anxiety that seems to surface its murky head. You know, the type your soul dredges up every so often to remind you there's no escaping it, no matter how much OM meditation you do.

On the surface it appeared I had the perfect life — a successful psychology career, a loving wife, a beautiful home and all the luxuries that come with living in Santa Monica. Beneath that rainbow however, there was no gold, just emptiness. I ended up with a failed marriage in which I lost not only my best friend, but also the life I'd known. The good life vanished, all of it, all except for Betsy, and my canine pal Blue.

"I don't want to be married anymore," Jill told me. "I don't want this life."

Jill and I were married for six years, but together since our first year at university. Every success and failure I experienced, I did so with her. Everything that mattered was attached to her somehow. And now it was floating away. The wind caught it when I wasn't paying attention and it was drifting beyond my reach. The life we'd built, the dreams for our future, all gone.

She stood and explained to me all the reasons that she couldn't stay. I only stared back at her and nodded my head. I wanted a good rebuttal—something that would convince her she was wrong. Fear and panic swelled in my belly. My skin burned hot and my head felt heavy. Any minute I knew my thoughts would spill out before her on the floor. I was crumbling, but still I couldn't bring myself to speak up.

I wanted her and the life we had come to know. Just thinking of me without her made life feel empty. But I had no good debate. My lips were paralyzed and my expression stayed blank. I felt a deathblow to my guts. Every part of me ached, but to her I was only nodding in agreement because I couldn't find my words. And so I let her go without putting up a fight.

I saw my very existence leave in a taxi that day. I felt real heartache—physically I felt it. My ribs squeezed my lungs and my blood vessels constricted. I was sure I could feel all of it. Then painful nostalgia swallowed me whole.

That wasn't the first time someone walked away. My mother was never around. She walked out on dad when I was just a child, almost 6 years old. She walked out on all of us.

Dad tried his best to raise us. He gave it a good go but eventually decided my sister and I would have a better life if Grandma Gladys and Grandpa Tad took care of us. And they did. They gave us everything they possibly could have. If generosity and love could undo hurt, theirs would have. Sometimes hurt is too big for anything.

What they could never give us back was a true sense of security. They could love us, feed us, and buy us train sets for Christmas. They could take us to football games and see us off to school every morning. They could not, however, make us whole again. When the other boys and girls cried for their moms and bragged about their fathers, my grandparent's affection fell short. I knew I was loved. But that love couldn't keep this faux friend called 'abandonment' at bay, who showed up one day out of the blue and decided to stay.

My grandpa died of a sudden heart attack when I was only eleven. His death was another reminder that I was not being raised by the people that brought me into this world. It reminded me that my parents weren't around. I sat in the church pews and stared at his gleaming casket draped with lilies. I thought not of him, but of my mother and father.

My grandmother died when I was in my early twenties. I was an orphan all over again. I was also in the throes of graduate school, scraping by to make ends meet. But by then I had Jillian. "We'll get through all of this," she assured me. "You'll always have me."

I thought my life struggles would help others. I thought I could help the world, heal those that were suffering like I was. So I became a psychologist. My goal was to mend the broken. I had no idea that there was more to treating human suffering than merely experiencing pain myself. I came in blind and a little arrogant. Life caught up to me and so here I am, a man running from himself, trying to find that elusive inner sanctuary so many speak of.

Standing on deck, I see the most awe inspiring image I have ever laid eyes on — the secluded island of Palmyra — a beautiful Pacific refuge bursting with untouched vegetation and wildlife. Bright colors of tropical fowl dot the canvas of a calm, blue sky long before I can reach the sands of the shoreline. This must surely be paradise.

The uneasy feeling I had down in the galley evaporates as we get closer. I will myself to let go of every thought that intrudes my mind. I rid myself of the mental chatter that dares interrupt the serenity of this scene.

I made it! The solitude of Palmyra is the whole reason for this voyage — to let go and find my inner peace.

Although the ocean is where I feel most alive, it has been quite some time since I severed myself from society in such a complete way. I'm a real Type A personality — a psychologist with scores of patients and social commitments. Between patient appointments, seminars, and teaching, I rarely have the time to slow down and evaluate what is going on with me. My packed schedule and constant diversions from my own life were on Jill's long list of reasons as to why she couldn't be with me. Not long after Jill left I realized that it was time to pause.

I became distracted at work. As patients told their stories, I sized them up to my own. They had no idea, but we were competing for best tragic life story. More often than not I won. There's no prize for that though.

"What do you think makes you feel that way?" I would ask each patient. But that is where I stopped comparing notes. That is where I abandoned my own issues. I would leave answering that question to my patients.

Around the same time I found myself struggling to keep my personal battle out of my profession the ocean started calling out to me. When the ocean calls you must answer, and it had been calling for over a year, as it tends to do when my life gets too chaotic. The ocean is as relentless as the past. It doesn't quiet down or let you go. So I took a sabbatical and here I am.

The breaking of the water tells me that I'll be ashore in no time now. I take a deep breath, and fill my lungs with the untainted salty air that surrounds me. I call to Blue to join me on the deck.

My head is now as unoccupied as the atoll that is spread out before me. I let the saline breath out of my lungs and make my way to the wheel. My four weeks at sea have been peaceful, but I'm happy to be reaching land again.

Betsy is a loyal companion, and probably the best boat I've ever had. She can be temperamental however when the wind picks up and a little rough when things don't go her way. So I'm ready for the solid, unmoving earth beneath my feet.

I ease Betsy into one of the two lagoons in the atoll. The island horseshoes around the lagoons, blocking the wind, so the waters are calm. Once I'm in as far as I can go, I drop anchor and cut the engine.

The islets surrounding the lagoon are even more breath-taking up close. The abundant forests and virgin terrain are so foreign to me that I am overcome with sentiment for this island haven. There is something other-worldly about this place. I feel like I've not only arrived at my Garden of Eden, but to a different era in time.

A strange disorientation of time and place penetrates my being. I stand quietly for a minute or two and take in the view. I feel blessed, both physically and deep within — maybe a natural effect of my surroundings. My body feels light and my head clear. That is something I can't recall feeling in some time. Palmyra is already working its charm. I am fully immersed.

I work past my goose bumps and get myself ready to explore. I prepare the dinghy to take to the shore; Betsy can't travel in water less than ten fathoms. I throw everything I'll need into the smaller boat and order Blue to "load up." He dutifully hops in the little boat and waits for me to join him. I run through my checklist to be sure I haven't left anything behind. Blue and I are off to Cooper Island. The sun warms my skin and awakens all my senses. The feel of the oars, the sound of the water splashing against the boat, the smell of the salty lagoon — all of it wraps me up completely.

When the lagoon bottom is only a couple of feet beneath me, I roll my pants to the knees, hop into the tepid water and pull the little schooner onto the sandy beach. Blue has already abandoned ship and is running in the surf, snapping playfully at the incoming tide. The unfamiliar sounds of the island stir up uncomfortable emotions as I disembark my little vessel to set up camp.

As my feet hit dry sand, I cup my hands over my eyes and survey the shoreline to scout out a good campsite. I figure Blue and I will spend most nights in Betsy's belly, but I want to have a site set up as well. To sleep on the sand under the stars makes me feel at one with the world, so I'll pitch a tent and make a fire pit not too far from the beach.

It doesn't take long to find my spot, an area that isn't inside the vegetation of the forest, but is close enough that a few towering coconut trees provide some shade. From here I can see Betsy and can keep an eye on her. I want to be sure she is safe even though there is no one on the atoll but me.

With coconut trees to protect me from the harsh Pacific sun and a clear view of my beloved, I drop my belongings and hastily build a modest campsite. I break into a hard sweat digging a fire pit and pitching my tent. The physical activity is refreshing. I feel alive. It clears my mind even more. Working with my hands instead of my mind is a welcome respite.

I work fast so I can get to the fun stuff, exploring the rest of the atoll. The island itself is only a little more than four and a half square miles. I don't imagine that I can get too lost on my exploits, which is a relief to me.

With the camp site ready, I set out with my backpack full of supplies I'll need for the day — plenty of drinking water for me and Blue, dried fruit, some protein bars, jerky, a compass, and an economy-sized bottle of sunscreen.

As a kid my grandma was always a stickler for sunscreen. I carried that with me into adulthood. I pop the cap off and take a deep breath. The smell of sunscreen and salt water overwhelms me. I can almost feel my grandmother beside me. I am eight years old again and on the beach over a long weekend.

As I start my hike, it occurs to me how very odd it is to be in a place uninhabited by humans. This island has never been occupied, which drew me to it. Now that I am here, I realize how strange it is to be alone. After years of listening to the hardships and troubles of others, I take solace in the silence Palmyra offers.

This is exactly what I need.

I hike along the coastline and notice the sweet smell of Scaevola — the flowering plant that covers the island. I feel the damp air on my skin, and the drumming call of majestic frigate birds soaring above me on imposing wings. Off in the distance I notice red-footed boobies with electric blue beaks scattered along the shore. Blue stirs up trouble with the coconut crabs as we travel.

"Behave yourself, Blue," I say. His enthusiasm for new places makes me smile.

I trek my way along the sandy shore and make it to the other side of the lagoon. While doing my research, I read something about war ships that used the atoll as a place of refuge during World War II. I imagine massive ships sneaking into the lagoons and hiding in the thick groves of the palm trees. It occurs to me that I am also seeking refuge on the island, but from a different kind of threat.

Blue is now bored with the sand and the lagoon. He is ready to get into the thick of the island. I leave the shoreline and start for the dense forest before me. My eager companion sees me heading for the tree line and races to join me. Together, we're off to explore. I watch Blue's tail wag and feel my heart beating along with it.

There is nothing that indicates another person has set foot on the soil before me. I know that there have been people here at one time — military personnel, other voyagers like myself, and researchers — but I don't see any proof of that among the coconut and the towering, smooth-barked Pisonia trees that grow wild all over the island.

I walk without a destination, and spend the morning shaded by coconut palms as I meander along the turquoise lagoons, observing the splendor of the coral reef flats carpeting the horizon. As I ponder the reason for this uninhabited atoll, Blue disappears off in the distance.

"Blue!" I call after him. "Let's go, Blue!"

I stop and wait for him to reappear. Nothing. I call out again. This time I am stern. I rarely have to call him twice. I can feel panic building beneath my rib cage. Along with Betsy, Blue is the most important companion I have — one of the few things I still have. I take off after him. I cannot handle another loss. I cannot lose Blue in this foreign place.

Be calm, Lucas. He's just exploring. My thoughts bring little calm as my pulse pounds away throughout my body.

"Blue!" I holler into the trees as I trudge along at a near jog. My agitation increases and not just because Blue has gone missing. I come to an abrupt halt. A bristling sensation travels up my spine. Something is off; something is wrong. Suddenly, I hear barking off in the distance.

"Blue?" I yell.

I stop for a second and let out a breath. My chest loosens a bit and my thoughts slow down. The dread that was enveloping me starts to ease up some and I try to follow the sounds of Blue's frantic barking. I continue to call out as I jog toward his howls. I know Blue well; I can tell he isn't hurt. But he is making quite a fuss. He's obviously come across something he feels needs my attention.

Blue's barks grow louder and more intense as I trot further inland. Knowing I'm headed in the right direction, I quit calling his name to listen. I can tell that he is standing still, wherever he is. By the sound of his howls, Blue has to be close. I start to run, and then stop hard.

Before me is a cave. Blue is inside. I take a few steps forward without saying a word. I cannot see my noisy companion yet, but I know he is close.

"Quiet, Blue," I order as I stand at the entrance of the cave.

My eyes trace the walls and ceiling of the stone chamber Blue has discovered. The place is beautiful. The walls are encased with an opal-like crystal—some mineral I've never seen before. The crystal collects every scintilla of light that enters the cave and twinkles against the dark that surrounds it. It's mesmerizing.

I take several steps forward and feel the ground give way beneath me. My own shouts fill my ears as they bounce off the walls of the cave. My body feels weightless. Time is rushing by and barely moving simultaneously.

Everything is dark. I'm choking on my own heart as I blindly grab for any roots or a rock—anything that will stop me from falling deeper into whatever it is.

I'm going to die in here. This is it.

Finally, I slam to the ground. I must have stumbled into some kind of chasm. I feel something warm and damp on my face. I still can see nothing, but I know something is near me.

Am I blind? Am I conscious?

The warm, damp sensation moves to my left hand, then my right. The warmth fades and I hear something. It sounds like whining. I can hear, but I can't see. I can feel earth beneath me, but I don't know how far I've fallen or how to get out. Fear and darkness gulp me up. I feel claustrophobic within them—like I cannot escape.

I cannot collect myself enough to figure out what is going on. It's too dark. I have no idea where I am now or how I am going to get back to the ground above.

Breathe, Lucas. Concentrate.

Slowly my eyes come into focus and begin to adjust. My head starts to come clear and I can see I'm in the exact same spot I was when I fell. That warm sensation is Blue's tongue on my skin. I didn't tumble down some hole at all. I must have passed out for a moment. Weird, I never have fainting spells.

I pull myself up to my feet and brush the floor of the cave off my clothes. Blue isn't paying attention to me anymore. He's staring into the cave, a guttural sound coming from deep inside his body. The hair on his neck is bristled. The muscles in his neck are tense.

"What is it, Blue?" I whisper as I put a hand between his shoulder blades. I feel his skin twitch under my palm.

"I think it's me," I hear echo from within the cave.

Again I nearly choke on my own heart. My breath is caught behind it. I suck in a gulp of air and swallow hard. All the blood in my body drains to my feet. It's balmy and warm even in the cave, but I feel a chilly breeze hit my exposed skin as I try to figure out what it is I just heard.

"I think I've startled the both of you," the voice says.

3

W hat in the hell is going on? I can't possibly be hallucinating from lack of social contact so early in my journey! It took Chuck Noland much longer than this to start talking to a volleyball.

"You can hear me, can't you?" I hear the voice say, and it seems to be getting either louder or nearer to me.

I can see nothing inside the cave save the sparkling of the minerals. I squint to find the owner of the voice and I clutch the knife hanging in its sheath from my belt. That is something my grandfather taught me. Never go anywhere without a good knife.

"Who's there?" I call into the cave. "I'm a—I'm armed," I stutter. I can hear my voice shake as it bounces in the cave.

"Hello there."

A man appears holding his hands in front of him to show me he isn't a threat. He's a little over six feet tall with drowsy hazel eyes and a round face that looks perpetually juvenile. I can tell he's well into his thirties despite the baby face. There are laugh lines at the corner of his tired eyes and I can see the permanent markings of his facial expressions etched into his forehead.

"I'm Edmund," he introduces himself and waits for me to speak. I just stand looking at him so he goes on. "I guess you just got in."

I stand for what feels like weeks as I try to figure out who this man is and what he's doing on Palmyra. He is obviously American; I can tell by his accent. I hadn't seen any indication that there could be anyone other than me on the island. The appearance of this Edmund is causing my brain to do flips in my skull. As far as I could see, there is only one part of the island that would allow for a boat to anchor—the west lagoon, in which Betsy is resting after her long trip. There is no way I could have missed another boat.

After a long pause I decide I had better find my voice again and ask. Standing shocked and mute is getting me nowhere.

"I'm sorry to be so direct," I finally say, "but who exactly are you?"

The man looks at me with an amused grin. He sees the knife I'm clutching and takes a step back. I quickly let go of the knife and go on.

"It's just, I thought I was the only one here."

The mysterious man that seemed to materialize out of nothing is Edmund Fanning. He fancies himself an explorer and his enthusiasm is something to behold. Everything he says, he does so with the zeal of a freshly-reaped convert. He is on fire for life the way evangelicals are on fire for the Holy Scripture. It seems the wear and tear of everyday life robs most of us of such enthusiasm by the time we hit our thirties, so Edmund's gusto is a bit foreign.

"I've been here for years now," Edmund explains as we exit the cave. I nod in response. "That's why you don't see a boat anywhere."

"I had no idea people lived here," I tell him as I observe a chunk of the mineral from the cave in his hands.

"It filters water," he explains, lifting the mineral to eye-level.

"Ah."

"And in response to your assumption, I don't think that many people know we're here," he says with a smile.

"We?" I ask.

"Yes, we — plural," he answers.

"There are more?"

"Oh, sure," Edmund chuckles. "Did you think I was a recluse?"

"I guess I didn't think that far into it." I glance around to see if I can spot sets of eyes hiding within the foliage around us. All of a sudden an intense sense of unease creeps into me. It is that same troubled feeling I got when I was in the galley of the catamaran earlier in the day. I can't help thinking about this stranger and his gang slinking around the island. I am beginning to wish Blue and I were alone.

"They're not here," Edmund assures me, obviously in response to my eyes scanning the forest.

"Oh, sure," I mutter.

"And if you're worried about being rampaged, robbed, or taken advantage of in any way, don't fret."

"I wasn't," I reply quickly.

"Really," he goes on. "Everyone here came for peace and quiet and nothing else. We all actually wound up here at different times and have formed a tight-knit community."

Again Edmund waits for my response, but I stand quietly trying to take it all in. I glance at him and down at Blue. I scan the island. My mouth curves into a frown and my eyes narrow. I hate it when wrenches are tossed into my pans. And Edmund seems to be a wrench.

"We don't think of ourselves as owners of this place and we don't see those coming to visit as trespassers."

"I suppose that's a good…"

"We aren't pirates or thieves," Edmund interrupts me. "We are just people looking for a fresh start and a new outlook on life."

"Sounds familiar," I say trying to soften my expression.

"Like everything on this island, we do not harm anything that is not out to harm us."

"Okay then," I mumble. "Nice to have met you I guess."

I turn from Edmund to go about my day. Blue catches up to me and I let my hand fall to rest between his ears for a moment as we walk. I take a cleansing breath and try to gather myself. Edmund's presence makes my shoulders tense and clutters my peacefulness. It almost offends me that he is here. I know he was here before I was, but I feel *he* is the intruder.

I've travelled all this way to get some peace, and here I am with some tourist group with their own baggage.

I stop and turn to face Edmund again. I will not let these people ruin my sabbatical. I will not let this stranger invade my time.

"So is there anywhere I can go that isn't inhabited?"

"Sure," Edmund answers.

"Could you tell me where?"

"I suppose…"

"Not to be rude," I interject. "But I kind of came here for solitude."

"We're mainly just on the main island, on Cooper," Edmund answers almost apologetically.

"Thanks then," I say as I turn to leave again.

"We didn't come all this way for a slumber party, did we," I say to Blue under my breath.

"If you change your mind, your welcome to join us," Edmund calls after me. I throw a hand in the air to let him know I heard him, but no thanks.

"We'll find our paradise yet," I say to Blue. "Why is everything such a chore, Old Blue?"

I know that Edmund is trying to ease my fears, but his attempt to convince me that he and his friends are peace-loving and friendly only exacerbate my anxieties about my new island mates. I have become accustomed to looking at others' straight-forwardness as a red herring, used to cover their true motives or disguise who they really are. I immediately assume that Edmund is setting some kind of trap.

"The island can be tricky," Edmund calls after me. "At least let me show you around a bit."

As perturbed and paranoid as I am with Edmund and his cohorts showing up to ruin my journey, I don't want to offend this man. I'm on a nearly deserted island with strangers after all. I turn around and force a grin, trying my best to convince Edmund that I trust him and that I'm not holding a grudge.

"I only want to help," he reassures me.

"I don't doubt that," I lie. It becomes clear to me, and probably to Edmund too, why I never took up acting.

"Hmmm," Edmund murmurs as he fixates on my face. "You still look a little guarded to me."

"Not at all," I reply, a little put off by his persistence.

"I want you to get the most from your time here."

"That's what I want too."

"Yes, well, it's a wonderful place and it has a lot to offer, so I'll do my best to assure you that there is no reason at all to fear anyone here on the island."

"Oh, I know that," I say nervously as I try my best to convince myself I mean it. There is not a reason in the world that I should not trust Edmund. He's done nothing what-so-ever to suggest he is anything but an honest man. As I sit and ponder over my instinctive doubts of others, I begin to realize that I have some serious work to do in the trust department.

Perhaps it isn't a trust issue, I think. Perhaps it's a survival instinct telling me to run!

As I grapple with the two notions I have concocted in my mind; one, that I have some serious trust issues, and the other that I am simply paying attention to my natural instincts, Edmund begins to talk again.

"If we had any plans to maim you or hold you up, rest assured we would have done it by now," Edmund tells me with a pat on the back and a congenial smile.

He seems to be digging his hole deeper by the second. Now I am really second-guessing his motives. One thing I have learned well from life is that often when a person expends a decent amount of energy to tell you how good they are, it is because they have spent double that doing bad.

Edmund shifts his weight and cocks his head to one side. He looks past me and says, "I think trying to convince you of who we are is working against me." It is like he read my mind. "My intentions are only to make you feel comfortable, but it appears I'm failing at that."

"Oh, well," I start to speak but he keeps going.

"I think that the only way that I can prove to you who I am, and who my friends are, is by letting you meet us and come to your own conclusions."

"I don't know if that's necessary," I insist. I can't think of anything else I'd rather do less at the moment.

"Sure it is!" he replies. "I'm a stranger, after all. You don't know me from Adam, so why trust me?"

Edmund is right. I have no idea who he is, or if Edmund is even his name. There is no reason for me not to trust him, but there is also no reason for me to believe anything he says. It comes down to a leap of faith. And when it's all said and done, with all my doubts and anxieties, I cannot help but to go ahead and believe that he's being honest with me. I am a psychologist, so I have an eye for the mentally ill and deranged. Edmund doesn't seem to have any of the tell-tale signs of a lunatic. I try to take comfort from this fact.

I do not want to spend any more time with Edmund, or his friends. Not because I think he may kill me—not anymore anyway. I would rather go on about my day, as this wasn't on my agenda. Human relationships are the reason for my running. Because of that, Edmund is becoming a real thorn in my side. *You are being unreasonable and pig-headed.*

If life is a sequence of lessons, and if I'm here on Palmyra to learn, I'd be passing up an opportunity not getting to know Edmund. I push myself to accept this new thing I wasn't expecting. I push myself to step outside my comfort zone. I try to let myself enjoy this interaction instead of resenting it.

"It just occurred to me that you haven't told me your name yet," Edmund says, breaking the awkward silence. "That seems like an appropriate enough place to start this derailed conversation over."

"Lucas Newell," I tell him as I offer my hand to this interesting new acquaintance. "And this is Blue."

"Well, Lucas Newell," Edmund says smiling as he places his hand in mine, "it is a pleasure to meet both of you. What brings you to this lovely little paradise?"

"It's a little complicated" I start.

"I have plenty of time," Edmund replies.

"Well, let's see," I say, trying to figure out what kind of information I am willing to share with a complete stranger. "I'm from Santa Monica. I have a clinic there. I'm a psychologist."

"That sounds very interesting," Edmund says as he keeps his eyes locked on mine.

"It is," I agree. "But it can be tough — very draining at times."

"Of course," he emphasizes. "But fulfilling too, I suppose."

"Oh sure," I say.

"So I know your name, occupation and where you take up residence, but you still haven't said why it is you and Blue here set off by yourselves for an island you thought was uninhabited."

Edmund's candor is a little surprising to me. I'm so accustomed to people either running circles around topics or burying their feelings deep inside that I am at a loss as to how to respond to such frankness. I conclude I should simply meet his bluntness with bluntness.

"I'm a psychologist," I state as if I am stating a case in front of a jury, "and it occurred to me one day that I have no idea who I am."

"Really?" Edmund asks. "Isn't that one of life's greatest questions—Who Am I?"

"I suppose you're right," I agree. "Every day I see people and I tell them how to go about their lives, but I have no idea how to go about my own. I just started to feel like kind of a fraud I guess."

Wow. That was a little liberating. There, I said it. I said what it is I am running from.

"And so you decided to sail off to an island as an escape from that?"

"Not as an escape so much," I explain. "I would say a retreat."

"Did you tell your family and friends what you were doing before you set sail?" Edmund asks, still concentrating his attention on me.

"I did," I tell him. "I am actually keeping in contact with my closest friend—her name is Samantha. We chat at least once a week via my satellite phone. Every Sunday I call to check in and tell her how things are going."

"I assume this means you aren't married..."

"Right," I blurt.

"If you check in with a friend rather than a wife and kids."

"I was married actually, before—no kids though," I tell him.

"Oh?"

"Yeah, for years I was married, but it seems I'm better at mending relationships than being in them myself."

"I guess that goes along with the original problem," Edmund says thoughtfully, "about healing the world without living the experience."

"Indeed it does," I agree.

"So your friend, is she the only one you contact?"

"Regularly anyway."

"You aren't close enough to your family to feel the need to speak with them while you are on your voyage?"

"Well it's not that. It's. . ."

"You aren't afraid they'll worry if they don't hear from you?" Edmund cuts in again.

Edmund's questions are simple enough, but also profound. I feel like I am the patient and he has become my therapist. I cannot discern his intentions in asking these questions, but I am certainly beginning to see some things I had been missing for quite some time.

"I only have a sister really," I finally say.

"Oh," Edmund replies a little caught off guard.

"I guess because I lost everyone else I just don't make a real attempt to stay that close."

"I'm sorry," he apologizes and breaks eye contact.

"I actually go weeks, even months sometimes, without talking to my sister. It never even occurred to me to tell her how the trip is going."

"I hope I haven't overstepped there."

"No, it's fine," I say, and then finish my thought. "We just don't keep in touch. We're busy with our own lives, you know."

"I'm sure she'd be interested in something like this," Edmund pushes the topic. "Even if you don't talk much regularly."

"I guess she would," I admit.

"You don't think it's strange to be so distant from your own family?"

"It's just what I've always known," I tell him. "I don't feel that we're distant. We just aren't close. That's easy for me."

"Tell me if I'm being too familiar," Edmund says.

"Really, you're fine," I assure him. "It's good to think about these things. You bring up good points; some things that I failed to see myself. It often takes an outsider to see something vital you've missed."

"I'm sincerely interested," he tells me. "Obviously, I've come here myself, so there is no judgment attached to any of my questions; only curiosity."

"Absolutely," I say. "Your questions made me think, though. When I left, I didn't think it at all strange that I intended to keep in touch with only one person. Now I'm starting to see that as problematic."

"My intentions weren't to make you feel guilty," Edmund says apologetically. "I was just trying to understand."

"No need for apologies," I assure him. "I thought I was coming to a deserted island to figure some things out. I'm beginning to think that solitude is really the last thing I needed."

"Solitude can be a real gift," Edmund says. "It allows us to refocus and embrace our whole-self, yet we must live in a balanced way with others. I know this may sound odd, coming from a man who lives with a handful of others out in the middle of the ocean, but to me relationships of all forms are an amazing way to grow as individuals. Our connections are fundamental to the way we understand ourselves and the world around us."

"Life just gets so chaotic with others around," I say.

"But most of our chaos comes from within, don't you think?"

"You've not been stuck in L.A. traffic recently. That is undoubtedly external chaos."

"I can't say that I have," he admits, grinning. "But I think you know what I mean."

"I do," I admit. "I just thought getting away from everything could help give me some perspective."

"Perhaps so."

"I don't want to sever all my ties with others. I just want some quiet time to get to know the real me."

"Well, that's a grand reason for your stay here on Palmyra," Edmund says, which makes me a little less defensive. "This is the perfect place to cleanse your mind!" Edmund laughed, startling some birds nearby.

"I can see why." I look around the island, captivated again by its beauty. "This place is amazing. Untouched by the world."

"It truly is," Edmund agrees. "And I bet that you'd like to see the rest of it now that you've realized I'm not a menace. I'd be happy to tell you all I know. Let's make our way towards our retreat so you can meet the others."

4

Mentioning the others rekindles some of my anxiety. Having met Edmund has thrown me for a loop as it is. I'm a bit nervous about having to go through more introductions. I have my reservations about sharing the reasons I've come here with more strangers. Besides, I'm outnumbered.

I get past my reluctance. After all anyone who has been in contact with such an insightful person as Edmund can't be too bad. I follow Edmund back into the lush foliage. Blue trails along behind us, sniffing furiously at everything new around him.

I can tell that Blue is no longer threatened by Edmund. I take that as a good indication of Edmund's character. Blue's instincts are spot-on. I trust Blue and Blue seems to trust Edmund. I think of my ex-wife, a manipulative woman with an aura of negativity. Blue never liked her, regardless of her attempts to win him over. I guess Blue could tell better than I could how her energy was draining mine.

"Edmund, have you been in love?" I ask.

"No beating around the bush," Edmund replies with a smile. He turns to look at me. "Indeed I have, Lucas. My love is still with me, just not here on Palmyra."

"When will you see her again?"

"She comes to visit sometimes, but this isn't her home."

"Oh?"

"Life is about choices, Lucas, and although others may walk alongside us, our path is one we walk alone."

I feel like I've been teleported to an ashram in India.

Edmund continues. "There are many things you will learn here. Just as in life, the lessons will come at their own time."

"What if I don't know the lessons I need?" I ask, trying to figure out just where Edmund got his psychic insight.

"Sometimes we are shown the path without ever asking a question; and sometimes we are not given answers, but are shown the way to find them," he replies.

"I guess you're right."

"Come this way," Edmund says as he nudges me.

We head through a tangle of branches hanging low with huge, vibrant leaves and stomp through the sprawling Scaevola that covers the forest floor. I see bundles on top of bundles of these white half-flowers reaching for the sun as we trek through the jungle-like viscera of the atoll.

Edmund suddenly stops and bends over. I am busy gazing around at the scenery instead of watching what my guide is doing, so I nearly slam into the back of him. Coming to a halt, I look down to see what he's reaching for. Edmund comes back up with a few young coconuts cradled in his arms.

"What do you say we rest a bit and enjoy some of what the island has to offer?"

"I don't see why not," I agree. "It's not like we're on a tight schedule."

We veer off the path to find a good place to settle down. I call out to Blue, so he knows that we have stopped. We find a nicely shaded area, plop down, and Edmund breaks open the coconuts. He hands me half of one as he puts his half to his mouth and tips it up. I do the same with mine. The coconut water tastes fantastic—like nothing you could find in any health food store back home.

"Wow," I say after gulping the contents. "That's really refreshing. It quenches thirst better than ice cold water."

"Indeed it does," Edmund says with a smile in response to my excitement. "Coconut water is great for hydration because of the electrolytes, and is packed with vitamins and minerals." This island has everything you could ever need."

"I feel like I've had an internal spa treatment!"

As we enjoy our drink, I see that Edmund's eyes are fixed on something in the distance. I squint to focus my vision as I try to follow his gaze. I am a little startled to see a man about 100-yards from us sitting on the ground. He is resting his back against the trunk of the Pandanus tree, a palm-like tree indigenous to the atoll that are sixty feet tall and have strap-like leaves that are the size of grown men.

I look on further and see that not far away from the man is a small house—a shack really. It's tucked back in the trees and barely noticeable. It looks to be made of cement blocks. I imagine something once used to shelter servicemen.

My muscles tense and my heart beats a little faster than usual. "Are we in trouble?" I whisper.

"Not at all!" Edmund says. "That's Captain Sawle. That little house you see is his daytime getaway."

Even Blue seems intrigued by the figure off in the distance. His hair bristles a bit, but he doesn't growl. We watch the captain quietly. He appears to be writing. As we study his outline against the backdrop of the jungle, the shadows that surround him seem to dance on the undergrowth as the fronds of the magnificent Pandanus sway in the tropical breeze.

The longer I stare, the more he looks like a vision than a real person. I blink hard and readjust my eyes. I think I must be too far off to see things correctly, because it looks as though the captain is writing on a sheet of bark. How archaic. Like something straight out of the nineteenth century. He must be sentimental. Or maybe there isn't any paper on the island.

Out of the corner of my eye I see Edmund stand up and brush himself off.

"I guess now is as good a time as any to introduce you," he says.

"Absolutely."

Together, we head toward the captain and his little hut. When we're about fifty yards away, Edmund calls out. I am a little surprised that he didn't notice us before, but I figure he was likely lost in whatever it is he's writing. As soon as the captain sees the two of us approaching, he puts the scroll down and tucks it to the side. The way he quickly shoves the scroll aside reminds me of a teenager hiding an embarrassing love note from his buddies.

"Good day, Captain," Edmund chirps as we get closer. The captain stands up to greet us. "This is a new adventurer who's just landed."

The captain looks at me and nods his head. I smile and nod back.

"He goes by Lucas and hails from California."

"Well, it is nice to meet a fellow explorer!" Captain Sawle reaches out to shake my hand.

He has kind, gray-green eyes, and looks to be a serious man. He's tall and stout and the deep-set wrinkles around his eyes and along his neck show the years he's spent in the sun the way a tree's rings tell its age. He's wearing old-fashioned sailor's pants and an undershirt with shoes he must have stolen from some museum. For a moment, I feel as if I've landed in some kind of nautical play. I want to call him Ishmael something awful, but I refrain. His dated attire aside, the captain has a dignified air that makes a person respect him. I may have just met him, but I get the feeling that he is much wiser than his years.

"Likewise," I tell him as we shake hands.

"Since you all are here, would you like to join me as I make my rounds in the garden?"

"I would love to," I say.

"Right this way," he says as he walks to the east side of the shelter where the garden is.

We get to the captain's charming little plot where he begins to explain all the herbs and native plants we're looking at. He has rows of the Ochrosia plant and the Moringa tree, which he tells me is also called the Miracle Tree. He pulls aside the vines that have entangled one of them and explains its many uses.

"The reason they call it the Miracle Tree is because of all its benefits," Sawle says as he pulls a few leaves off a branch. "These leaves have a great deal more Vitamin C than the best orange, four times more calcium and more protein than milk. It also has more potassium than a banana. It's a power plant. I've heard it said that it can heal hundreds of *dis-eases*. It gives anyone who eats it strong immunities and it's a great source of energy. I'll be sure to send some with you when you leave. If the world were to discover this plant, there would be no need for an apothecary anymore."

"I think that has already happened," I tell him, poking a little fun at the captain's reference of such an antiquated profession. He either doesn't get my joke or doesn't find it comical, because he says nothing in response. A little embarrassed, I clear my throat and we both pretend that I've said nothing.

While I'm impressed with the Miracle Tree, I cannot help but be distracted by the extraordinary collection of artifacts and relics that litter the captain's place. All around us I see the relics of a bygone era — things that you would find in the captain's quarters of an ancient sailing ship.

I cannot believe that the captain doesn't spend as much time describing these artifacts as he does discussing the plant life. All I can figure is that he has a soft-spot for horticulture and natural remedies. Even if he dabbles in botany, I'm surprised that a ship's captain wouldn't be more intrigued with the historical sailing objects that lay strewn about.

"Aren't you as mesmerized by these relics?" I finally ask the captain when I can no longer take it.

"They are interesting enough," Sawle replies, still looking at his beloved tree. "But those are things of the past. This Miracle Tree, however, is something that is here and living right now. And it offers its gift to keep all of us living and well in the present."

"I see what you mean," I tell him, "but I would think a captain like yourself would be fascinated with all this history."

"I appreciate history for what it has to tell us about our present. Those relics have taught me all I can learn from them. These plants though, are something here in the moment. They benefit me right now. The relics had their time."

"That's an insightful way to look at things. If my patients could see things the way you do, they would be healed, or at least on their way. You're saying live in the moment, yes?"

"Precisely," Sawle proclaims. "We should appreciate that which makes this moment good. The Miracle Tree makes us *feel* good today, and isn't today the best thing we have? This moment right now... *this* is ours."

"I suppose it is," I agree. "I could probably skirt many sleepless nights if I adopted that notion."

"Are you a doctor?" the captain breaks in.

"He's a psych... psychiatrist," Edmund answers for me with a stutter.

"I'm a psychologist," I interject politely. "I don't usually encourage the use of drugs, I go with the healthier approach, a more holistic way of healing."

"That's interesting," the captain says. "I think I'd like such a profession."

"It can be very fulfilling," I reply. My attention is diverted by a large ship's bell. Its inscription reads "1802." Next to the bell I see the scroll Sawle put down when we arrived. That reminds me of his writing.

"What are you working on, Captain?" I ask nodding toward the scroll.

"Oh, just my thoughts about life."

Edmund seems a little alarmed by my question. He rushes over to me, leans into my right ear and whispers, "Lucas, the captain is a private man."

I nod and let the subject float off into the warm island air. The moment seems a little tense until Edmund says, "Come now; we best be on our way."

"It was a pleasure to meet you, Captain," I tell Sawle.

"And you," the captain says with a nod.

"Let's go, Blue." Edmund and I leave the captain to get back to his private writing and continue our tour of the island. I wait until we're out of earshot to ask, "Where did all those artifacts come from?"

"From an old shipwreck that washed up onshore," Edmund says.

"That's some pretty great stuff," I reply. "A museum would kill for it."

"I think it's better suited to the island, though," Edmund says thoughtfully. "How long did you say you were planning to stay?"

"I hadn't said," I answer. "But I'll probably be here four weeks or so. I plan to visit a few islands in the South Pacific before heading home. Other than that, my plan is to have no certain plan."

"I like that plan," he calls back over his shoulder."

"It seems to have worked well for you," I say. "You have a good aura about you."

"That is very kind of you, Lucas Newell," my guide says as he stops so that we are face to face again. "You have a spark within you that can *light* this world; It's your choice to make it shine."

"I hope to by the end of this, anyway."

"You most certainly will," he reassures me and continues on his way again.

"How long is it to our destination?" I change the subject.

"It's not too far now," he tells me. "I don't know who will be there at this time, but at very least you can see our retreat."

"Sounds like a plan," I tell him.

"I don't mean to keep coming back to this," Edmund starts. "But once you're finished with your soulful endeavor, do you plan on returning to your practice and all that?"

"Most definitely" I tell him. "One of my reasons for coming here was to find something I feel I've lost. There seems to be parts of me that I have locked away inside me; that have been drowned out by the pain of my past, or that I have just completely severed. I want to find those pieces of myself again. I cannot do myself or any of my patients any good if I don't work on the voids in my own life."

"Sounds like sound logic," Edmund says.

"Before embarking on this journey, I remember standing in my garden one evening, looking up to the heavens; it was just me, the twinkles of the stars, and the darkness of night. I asked the Universe three questions—and prayed the answers would come to me; at the very least be guided towards where I needed to be in order to find them." I say.

"What did you ask?"

"Who am I? Why am I here? What is my meaningful contribution to this life?" I respond.

"Deep questions," Edmund replies.

"Yes, they are, aren't they?"

"You think that God will answer them?"

"I certainly hope so."

"I'm sure if you keep asking, the answers will come. I believe the verse goes: *Ask, and it shall be given; seek, and ye shall find; knock, and it shall be opened*, right?"

I smile at him and look up to the sky. There is something about being on a deserted island that makes it easy to divulge anything and everything to a complete stranger. There is something about Edmund that makes that feel okay. How nice it would be if my patients would open up and spill their beans without prodding or a prayer. That's a mess I would be willing to clean up.

"It sounds to me as if you've experienced a crisis of consciousness," my new friend suggests, startling me out of my thoughts.

"Or a midlife crisis," I joke. "But I'm only thirty-eight, so I guess I'm just an early bloomer."

"A mid-life crisis?" Edmund parrots the phrase.

"Sure," I said. "You know, when you hit the middle of your life and start to panic that you have no idea what you are doing or what life is about. But still you get older by the day, and you don't like it. Some men buy sports cars, but I guess sailing into the Pacific is more my cup of tea."

"That sounds awful—not the sailing into the Pacific, but the crisis itself," he says warmly. "I suppose I never had one because I have tried to seize life at every opportunity."

"That is one way to avoid them."

"I suppose it is, but I have never been afraid of my age or my level of success, really. I am only afraid of being boring or bored," Edmund adds.

"That is your only fear in life?" I ask, amused by the very idea that boredom could be one's biggest fear.

"I suppose I have a few others, but I think that is my biggest."

I look over at him as we continue to march through the trees and overgrown vegetation. I have never met someone like Edmund Fanning before. He seems too original. I have known him less than a day, but I can see that as clearly as I can see the coconut trees in front of me.

"Here we are," he says as we approach a compound with a few small, two-person bungalows, surrounding a concrete building in the center. Edmund tells me the building collects rainwater for the inhabitants to use for bathing and cooking.

"These were built by researchers not too long ago. Now that they are abandoned, we have taken up residence in them."

"What if the researchers return?" I ask.

Blue is darting in and out of the bungalows and I start to call for him, but Edmund stops me.

"He'll be fine," he assures me. "They have dirt floors. What can he hurt?"

I let Blue go about his exploring and return to our conversation.

"So?" I ask. "If the researchers need these again?"

"I guess we'll just have to deal with that if and when the time comes," the upbeat islander says with a smirk. "For now, we are the residents even if it's temporary; it's all ours."

"Fair enough," I say. "So where is everyone; besides the captain, I mean?"

"I guess out gathering food. We can go do the same while we wait if you'd like."

At this I heave my backpack from my shoulders and drop it to the ground. I unzip the bag and reach my hand down into it, coming back with a few protein bars and some dried apricots. I also take Blue's water bowl out that I always carry with me and give him some jerky.

"No need," I tell him.

"Aren't you the prepared one, Mr. Newell?" he says as he takes one of the small bags of dried apricots. "I'm not sure about those others though," he says pointing a finger at the foil wrapped bars.

"The protein bars?" I ask.

"Is that what they are? Yes, the protein bars. I guess I've just been on the island so long that I prefer things with only one ingredient," he says as he munches his apricots.

"These are great," I insist. "They have close to thirty grams of protein per bar and they're chalked full of vitamins and minerals."

"I don't know that I need so much in one food," he jokes. "I'll stick to the apricots, thank you. There is nothing worse than getting a rotten stomach in a place like this."

"Suit yourself," I say as I tear the wrapper off the bar with my teeth.

"I guess I will," he smiles. "What do you say we go exploring the island a bit more once you get all that protein in you?"

"Absolutely," I say with a mouthful of the chewy chocolate flavored bar. I see that Edmund is less than impressed with my meal-on-the-go bars. Every bite I take, he stops to watch me. It's as though he is watching someone eat a live frog.

"You sure you don't want one?" I ask again, knowing well what his answer will be.

"Very," he assures me.

I finish my lunch, hoist my backpack up to my shoulders again, and Edmund and I take off into the bowels of the island. He assures me he could maneuver the place in the pitch black without ever stumbling over a rock or bumping into a tree. I hope that he is as capable as he is confident. The further we go inland, the thicker the flora becomes. It's disorienting.

I watch my guide thrashing at the underbrush with a dull machete. He stops every ten feet or so to explain a plant or an insect along the way. I feel that I am, in fact, in good hands. He could fill an encyclopedia with what he knows about Palmyra. I wonder exactly how long he has been on the island to have learned it so thoroughly.

We are on the east side of the atoll now, not quite to the shoreline; near Papala Island. Edmund explains he wants me to be very familiar with the lay of the land. At the moment, we're headed to find what my guide claims to be the most delicious berries I will ever taste in my life. He tells me the colors alone are like nothing I've seen, and the taste is even more intense than the colors.

As we hike through the thick foliage, I notice something that stands out among the various vibrant greens that surround us. There is a little old shack about fifty yards from me, all but hidden in the foliage. I call out to Edmund, who's a ways in front of me, and veer off toward the tiny, broken-down abode.

I don't wait for Edmund to explore my find. I have to put my body weight against the door to get it to move. Inside, there are a few rusted chairs, a crudely-made table the size of a small card-table, and some shelving against two of the walls. The entire place consists of just one room.

As I look around, I see something beneath the table; it looks like an old wooden chest. At first I am surprised to see something that suggests an inhabitant, but I soon realize this is only a man-made structure. Someone must have lived here.

I can't help but wonder how long it's been since someone stepped foot inside. Who did the chest belong to? Why did they leave it behind? I kneel down and pull the wooden box out from beneath the old table. There is a lock, but it is so eaten with age that all I do is pull the clasps apart and the box opens. This tiny house and this chest have been here for a very, very long time.

I throw the lid back and inspect the contents. Just as I make my way through the first layer of yellowed photos and documents, I hear Edmund step inside.

Poring over the documents, I can see they are so aged as to be nearly illegible. Many of them are written on the same kind of scrolls that the captain was using. He must have found some of the old parchment lying around the island and decided to make use of it. Perhaps he loves the past more than he claims.

I lay the documents aside and pick up the photos. In one of them I see a man who looks familiar. Astonished, I look up at Edmund, who is now standing above me. The man in the photo could be his identical twin.

"This looks just like you Edmund." I hold the photo out to him. "If I didn't know better, I would say this is you."

Edmund takes the photo and glances at it for a moment, and then says, "Oh, I don't think any of these men look that much like me."

I take the photo back from him and study it more closely. Edmund must be blind if he can't see the resemblance.

It's eerie. The man is standing with a few other men in front of a ship on the island. They are all on Palmyra. I can't make out the date written on the back; its too faded and the lighting inside isn't ideal.

Edmund seems restless as I rummage through the trunk. He isn't at all interested in the place or the contents of the chest. I ask if he wants to look at more of the photos and he declines.

"It's probably best to leave things as they were," he suggests as he edges toward the door. "What do you say we get on to the berries?"

I can see that Edmund is uncomfortable, so I place all the photos and papers back into the trunk and secure the lid. While Edmund has his back to me, I quickly slip a few of the photos into my backpack. It's clear to me that the owner of the trunk and its contents is no longer living, so I see no harm in taking a few mementos. These photos have been on the island for ages without anyone claiming them. If no one has missed them so far, I figure they won't miss them now. Mounted and framed, they'll look perfect in my office back home. Besides, I want to study the Edmund look-alike a bit longer and see how much the man resembles my new friend, when I have some decent light.

By the time I replace the chest and step outside, Edmund is already a few yards away from the shack. Blue is standing near him; he refused to come into the hovel and he is acting strange as he paces.

I join them and we continue on our walk. Edmund picks up right where we left off, guiding me through the island and telling me everything he knows about the atoll. I only pay half attention; I am thinking more about the photos and how I need to call Samantha to tell her about everything I've stumbled upon that day. As distracted as I am, I know that my guide is likely saying something interesting or important, so I tune back in.

"People say there is something supernatural about this place," he explains as he slings his machete at an overgrown plant in our path. "From the time it was founded by a captain back in the late 1700's up until the twenty-first century, there have been rumors of strange occurrences on the atoll."

"What kind of strange occurrences?"

"Well the legend goes that when it was first discovered, the captain who stumbled upon it woke up three times in the night. The third time, he decided that his waking up must be a premonition of some sort, so he had his first mate heave to. The next day, they realized they were only about a mile from the reef that separates the lagoons, one of which is where your boat is anchored. They say if he hadn't stopped that night, they would have been shipwrecked."

As Edmund finishes his story, I feel chills race up my spine all the way to the crown of my head. I remember my own experience coming into Palmyra, the uneasiness I felt while standing in the galley that just wouldn't go away until I finally looked out to see the coral reef.

"You look a little pale, Lucas," Edmund says to me. "Do you need to eat?"

"It's not that," I tell him. "It's that story."

"What about it?"

"This may sound crazy, but I think the same thing happened to me coming in."

I explained to Edmund everything that had happened with my high-tech navigation going haywire, the nagging feeling I couldn't shake while I tried to make lunch, and the sudden appearance of the coral reef. He didn't seem terribly shocked by my story. He only nodded his head as I spoke.

"That's interesting," he finally says. "Maybe it's just a sailor's intuition."

"It seems so uncanny," I say as I try to gather my bearings. "Don't you find it strange that the exact same thing would happen to two different men?"

"It's just how it was meant to be, I'd say" Edmund replied.

I seldom think of life events happening because they were meant to. Where's the science in that? As I reflect, I realize that unexplained or miraculous things do happen in life without explanation or spookiness attached. I see that all the time in my line of work. Maybe Edmund is right; maybe they're signs or reminders that we should embrace instead of question. I failed to notice the serendipity of the moment, on my way in. My heart still heard the message; it saved me.

"It's our perception of the real-world experiences that dictates our path. What we discern depends on what we make of things," he says.

"That's true," I agree. "It seems that the island is watching over those who come near it."

"I might agree with you, except that's not the only story tied to this island," he goes on. "Back in the seventies there was a wealthy couple from California who sailed out to the island on their private yacht, the Sea Wind. Weeks after the couple left for their voyage, a man and woman surfaced in Hawaii with the couple's yacht. The two were only tried for thievery at the time. They couldn't call it a murder because there were no bodies. Six years later, an old chest surfaced in the lagoon and in it were the remains of the older, wealthy woman. They were discovered by another yachting couple visiting the island. So, the man who had showed up with the yacht in Hawaii ended up going to prison for murder, his girlfriend was acquitted, and the island's eerie legacy continued."

"That certainly puts a damper on things," I confess. I stay behind my guide to avoid a machete to the chin, keeping an eye on Blue so he doesn't lose an eye to the blade. "I almost wish I hadn't heard that."

"That was decades ago," Edmund assures me. "Being a psychologist, I would assume you aren't a superstitious man, anyway."

"I wouldn't say I am, but still I'd rather not tell ghost stories while I'm out here on an island in the middle of the Pacific."

"We'll avoid any more of those then," he promises.

"How about we focus on the good stuff? That's what this adventure is about, right? Reigniting your flame and making you feel part of something great?"

"I don't know that I've ever thought of it that way."

6

E dmund and I spend the day going around the atoll. It consists of several small islets that are mostly connected, so he takes me from one to the next. He truly does seem to know every square inch of the atoll. It's as though he had molded it from coral himself.

"What's on the islet over there?" I ask when I notice that there is one area he's said nothing about.

"Nothing much," he tells me.

"That's surprising from someone who has told me the history of every living thing on the place," I can't resist a grin.

Edmund's eyes darkened. "I avoid going over there if I can," he confesses. "It's the one part of the island I don't like."

"Why?" I ask.

"There's just something about it," he says staring at Holei Island. "I've never liked the area. I feel like it may be evil somehow."

"Evil? How so?"

"Sometimes you just have feelings about things," he tells me. "There's a darkness about it; and my intuition tells me we should avoid that place."

"Do the others feel the same way?"

"I suppose they do," he sighed. "I suppose you will too, if you stay for any length of time. I imagine you will trek through it at least once, so you can make your own judgment when that time comes."

"Remember though, I don't fancy myself superstitious," I remind him.

"I think there is a difference between superstition and discernment," Edmund declares as he turns away from the island. "Besides the supernatural, the place is infested with sharks."

"Infested?" I echo.

"Yes," he confirms. "I should have said that earlier. I wouldn't suggest swimming too often if you want to keep your limbs. The ocean life around here can be vicious."

"Do they attack often?"

"Oh, I wouldn't say often. One of the others, Klara, seems to believe they only do so when people threaten them, but I try not to test that theory."

I look to make sure Blue is on land when Edmund shares this with me. I shudder to think of a shark snatching my best friend and tearing him to shreds. I hope there aren't any more unwanted surprises waiting for me.

"Cheer up, old boy," Edmund says. "They aren't going to swim up to shore. The place is still amazing, sharks and all."

"Between the marine life and that island that gives you bad feelings, I don't know if I've come to the right place," I tell him.

"Look at how fast you've turned negative. I thought we made a pact, you and me. I thought we were going to pick the good out of things."

"So we did," I admit.

"The sharks and the atoll are a very small part of a whole," Edmund lectures. "What do you say we go meet the others? That should lift your spirits. I want to get back before the sun sets anyhow."

"I thought that you could make it across this island in the pitch-black without stubbing your toe," I tease my guide as we start to hike back.

"I said I could," Edmund answers me. "But that doesn't mean that I should."

The change in Edmund's demeanor is palpable. First, it was the mention of the creepy island. Now, he seems to be rattled by the notion of the setting sun.

"You sound pretty serious about the dark," I say, hoping that he will say something to explain the sudden shift in mood.

"There are not many things that I am afraid of, Lucas. I told you that not even death scares me much, but the dark on Palmyra, especially over here, I would rather avoid."

Edmund is standing squared in front of me, his eyes on mine. "Please, Lucas, if there is one thing you do while you are here, stay with the group once the dark settles in. Or be sure you are back on your boat in the lagoon."

"Okay," I say, shocked by his persistence and the gravity of his words. "But why?" I ask.

"It's just best," he insists. "This is an island out in the middle of nowhere. Who wants to get lost in the dark?"

His mood suddenly brightens again, but I can see that he is holding something back.

"Is this another ghost story of yours?" I ask, half jokingly.

"Oh, I'm quite finished with spooky stories," he laughs. "Suffice it to say, it is just safest to get to camp before the sun goes down."

"It seems there are more rules to this island than I expected," I say. "But I suppose I can abide."

There's something about Edmund that makes me trust him. I don't know the cause behind his intensity, but I see no reason to test him or his advice.

"I think that you'll like our little group," Edmund says, trying to lighten the mood again.

"I'm sure I will," I agree. "Why don't you give me a quick rundown before we meet them so I'll know what to expect?"

"Splendid idea," he chirps. "Well, there is Klara, who is kind of the matriarch of the group. She's the one who feels the sharks are no real threat. She is the elder, but you'd never know it by watching her out and about on the island. She's an agile old broad and also the wisest person I know."

"She sounds pretty astounding."

"Oh, she is," he gushes. "I often wish she was my own grandmother. She's lost her own family, so I think that perhaps she sees herself as grandmother to all of us."

"That's terrible," I reply, referring to the fact that Klara has lost her family.

"Oh, it's not that I don't appreciate my own grand-mother," Edmund starts to explain. I cut him off before he can finish.

"Oh I'm sure you do, I mean that it's terrible she's lost her own family."

"It is, but she is strong. She used her experience to learn, grow, and heal others. Where some may be bitter, I think it only made her wiser."

I can see the admiration he has for Klara in the way he looks when he talks about her.

"Then we have Kalama and Johnson Wilkinson," he goes on. "They are a married couple who came here from

Hawaii. They aren't bad when you catch them alone, but they can be fierce if they're forced to spend too much time in one another's company."

"How strange that they'd sail off to an island together if their relationship is so volatile," I say, thinking aloud.

"Perhaps that's why they came, to try and mend what is broken. They've been here for some time, and I have seen little progress in that department. They're good people—just not good for one another," he explains.

"A common saga for many," I put in. "Relationships can be tough."

"I suppose they can be," Edmund says in that thoughtful way that I have already learned means he has an opinion on the matter.

"Maybe I can help," I offer. "Being a psychologist and all."

"This is a trip about you, Lucas," he reminds me. "Assist if you feel the need, but remember why you are here."

"I guess you're right," I admit. "We all need our down time. So, who else will I be meeting?"

"There's Dr. Judd. He's a missionary, a physician and a great storyteller. He's from Hawaii as well. I think you'll find him quite agreeable."

"It sounds like I will," I agree.

"Then there's Captain Sawle, whom you've already met. He is a little gruff, but he's a decent man and plays a vital role in our little club. He wound up shipwrecked on the island and just decided to stay."

"I suppose he has no family either then?"

"Nobody really knows about that," Edmund replies. "I've always felt if he wanted to discuss that, he would. Since he doesn't, I assume it's better left alone."

"I'm not accustomed to leaving unexplored emotional baggage alone, but I will do my best if the captain seems to be content with his secrets."

"He does," Edmund reiterates. "You may come to your own conclusions once he starts talking a bit, but I'll leave that to you two."

"Is that everyone?" I ask.

"There is also the shaman," he explains. "He was here before any of us arrived. He seems to exist on the outskirts of the group, so I tend to think of Klara as our rock—keeping us all together."

"So he's an outcast?" I inquire.

"Not an outcast, per se," he explains. "He just seems a little less—tangible—than the rest of us."

"Tangible? That's a strange take on someone," I say.

"It is, isn't it? I think you'll see what I mean once you meet him. He's an amazing man, but he has a mystic air—in a good way, of course. He doesn't live with us though. You'll have to go with someone to the south islets to meet him."

"He isn't afraid to be alone in the dark then?"

"He's a shaman," Edmund answers. "He doesn't have the same fears as regular folks. And like I said, he is different than us. You'll see what I mean when you meet him."

"I look forward to doing that," I tell my new friend. "That makes seven, counting you. So that is everybody?"

"That is everybody in our group," he answers.

"Is there another group?"

"Not a group, but we have reason to believe that there may be others lurking around from time to time."

"That's why you don't go out in the dark?"

"Part of it," Edmund offers, as vague as ever.

"You've never seen anyone though?"

"Not exactly," he admits. "But we have our reasons. Let's not worry about that. It's nothing, really, I'm sure. We've not been bothered in quite some time."

"Do you think my boat is safe?" I'm suddenly panicked thinking about Betsy sitting out in the lagoon all by herself.

"I don't think you'll have to worry about the boat," he assures me. "But I would try to check in. We'd better do that before we head back to Sky. We're actually not far from the lagoon, so it won't set us back too much."

"What's Sky?" I ask.

"Oh, that's the compound we were at earlier. We call it the Sky Lodge. When the tropical rains come in, it's like the clouds roll into us embracing our home. When they pass, they leave a message of Light — with a beautiful rainbow to greet us."

"Sounds amazing," I say. "I'd love to see that."

"It rains all the time here, so I'm certain you will. Now how about we check on your ketch?"

"I'd like that," I say as I take a deep breath. "That boat is my everything."

"The boat is?" my new friend asks with a raised eyebrow.

"Well, the boat and Blue," I correct myself and reach down to scratch Blue between the ears. He must have overheard Edmund talking about the dark and gotten spooked himself. He came running up as we were talking and planted himself at my feet.

"A dog and a boat," Edmund utters, lifting his eyebrows.

"It's not as materialistic as it sounds," I defend myself. "I love the sea and being on Betsy is a way that I can become a part of it."

"Betsy is what you have named it?" Edmund inquires. I can see something has piqued his interest.

"Yeah, after my first love," I explain.

"We're two peas in a pod," Edmund chuckles. "I had a Betsy myself."

"A love or a boat?" I ask.

"It seems one in the same for you. A boat," he says after his little jab.

"What are the odds?" I say, amused by the coincidence.

"Oh, I don't believe in odds," he tells me. "Only fate."

"Perhaps we don't share a pod after all. You and I are very different people. I count on statistics to make a lot of my decisions," I tell him. "But it looks like in our case that opposites attract."

"So it would seem," he agrees. "Now let's go check your Betsy and get back to the others before nightfall."

We make it to the shoreline in no time. As soon as my little ship comes into view I feel a wad of tension leave my chest. She is right where I left her and looks unmolested. I want to take the dinghy out just to be certain and to make sure everything is secure. I left her under the assumption that I was on a deserted island. I fear I may not have been as thorough in my inspection before I made my way to shore.

"You mind if we go out just to check?" I ask as I brace the little dinghy, anchoring my feet in the sand to prepare for a good push.

Edmund glances up at the sky to measure how much time we have left. "We do need to hurry."

"It will take no time at all," I promise. "I just want to double-check."

"I meant what I said about the dark," Edmund persists. "I'm sure that you locked up before you left her."

"I thought I was alone when I left," I explain as I thrust the little lifeboat in the water, thinking of killer sharks while I do so. "This will take five minutes, tops."

"If we don't get back, Lucas. . ." Edmund starts to say something and then stops himself. "I just don't know that you need to go check."

"That boat brings me joy. It allows me to live my dream, and is my only way back home," I say firmly enough to emphasize my point. "I promise we will get back before dark. Hop in."

Blue has already taken his place in the dinghy. I can see that Edmund is not thrilled with my plan. Thrilled or not, he gives in, helping me get the dinghy into the lagoon, and we make our way towards Betsy. His eyes are focused on the placement of the sun the entire time we travel. I don't know what it is about the dark that has him so spooked. He seems outgoing and fearless in every other way. Regardless, it's clear that there is something I don't want to run into, something waiting on the other side of darkness.

"Relax a little," I tell him. "We're nearly there."

"Oh, I know it's absurd." Edmund lightens up some as he answers. "An adventurer racing the sun. I just don't want the others to worry if I'm not back in time."

"Sure," I agree. "Here we are."

The three of us climb from the small lifeboat to the catamaran and I hurry around to check all the locks and make sure everything is secure. Blue does a quick inspection himself and laps some water from his bowl on the deck.

I'm meticulous by nature, I should have known that I wouldn't leave my Betsy vulnerable. I am glad to have the peace of mind. Besides, I'm still not completely sold on my new friend's theory that the dark is terribly threatening. I don't regret the extra trip out.

"Looks good," I smile. "Ready to head back?"

"Absolutely," Edmund says. "It looks like we have plenty of time, too. You could wrestle a shark really quickly if you'd like," he taunts.

"I may try that tomorrow. I'm too tired today. After you, sir." I wait for my fellow adventurer to climb aboard the small vessel that awaits. I hold Blue's collar so he doesn't knock Edmund into the lagoon. Blue is usually good about letting others in the boat, but he seems to hardly take notice that Edmund is climbing in. He must be excited to get back to land.

My newest companion begins to climb aboard the dinghy but just as he puts his foot down, he freezes. He quickly draws his foot back. The way he yanks his leg back to the deck reminds me of the way a frightened turtle pulls his head into his shell when it realizes that danger is nearby.

"What?" I ask.

"Shh," he shushes me, putting a finger to his lips and a hand on my chest to hold me back from the edge of the boat. He is that stranger again warning me about the dark rather than the adventurer I met in the cave. He seems edgy and spooked all of a sudden.

"What?" I insist again, unnerved by his sudden strangeness. He stands quietly, looking out at the shoreline, then down into the boat for another minute.

"I think we should rest here for the night," he says finally.

"Why?" I try to follow his gaze to see whatever it is that's making him act this way.

"It's just getting late. I think you might prefer to stay in a familiar place your first night."

"You said we had plenty of time," I remind him. "It won't be dark for a while."

"It's not that," he insists. "I just realized that you've been through quite a lot already today, what with meeting me unexpectedly and being dragged around the place. It might be a little overwhelming for you to be hauled away to meet a group of people and sleep in an unfamiliar place." Edmund pauses for a few seconds, then goes on. "We'll set out first thing in the morning to meet the others."

"I do prefer staying here for the night," I admit. "But I would like to know the real reason you want to stay here and why you were shushing me."

Edmund chuckles lightly. "I just thought I heard the Wilkinson's bickering off in the distance. I wanted to be sure to call out to them if they were coming to shore so they'd know not to worry about this mysterious boat floating in the lagoon."

"So you decided it wasn't them, then?" I ask.

"No, it wasn't them. It was probably just some red-footed boobies squawking at one another. That's what they sound like sometimes," he laughs.

"Fair enough." I'm not completely convinced by Edmund's explanation, but trying my best to buy it. "Won't your friends worry? You said that you wanted to get back so they wouldn't worry."

"They know that I'll be safe. We try not to stay out all night, but it happens on occasion. They'll think I'm staying in the cave where you and I met. I do that occasionally when I am gathering the crystals."

"You're sure they won't think anything about you just not showing up?"

"Come now, Lucas," he slapped me on the back. "A man floating around the ocean who contacts a friend only on Sunday is suddenly concerned about how others may worry?" He is jovial, but still makes a sound point, so I drop it.

"Touché."

"Now, I hope you have more than those gooey protein bars to eat in the kitchen," he says as he turns and heads for the living quarters. "I'm starved, but not starved enough to have a go at one of those."

"I do indeed," I tell him as I walk past him to unlock the door that leads to the small living area on the boat.

I unlock the saloon door, flip on the light, and step aside to let my guest lead the way. He blinks hard in the florescent light. He looks like he's never seen electricity before. I imagine it has been a while, since he has abandoned civilization and all its modern conveniences.

"Have a seat," I insist as I make my way for the small pantry in the kitchen. I rummage through my cabinets for a simple evening meal and find some canned asparagus and a couple of cans of tuna. "How's this?" I ask.

"Perfect," he smiles. "And we don't even have to bait a hook."

"It's like I've pulled you back into the twenty-first century," I tease.

"It is indeed," he replies.

I heat the tuna and asparagus on the stove and serve dinner. Once we are finished, I pour both of us a glass of wine and we go back up to the deck to play a game of chess before the sun disappears for the night. As we are playing, the sun lowers into the ocean, and I notice a thick fog descend onto the island.

"I guess we should call it a day and head in," I say once the only thing left of the sun is a warm, pink glow.

"I think that's a good idea," Edmund agrees peering out to the island.

7

I let Edmund stay in the bedroom and take the sofa in the main quarters for the evening. The other cabin is full of supplies, so there's no room to sleep there. He tries to convince me that he would be fine on the sofa, but I insist, since he is my guest, that he takes the bed. I don't tell Edmund, but I'd rather stay in the living room anyway, so I can call Sam to tell her about my day. I've always hated to have conversations with others in the room so I'd rather call her when I have some privacy.

Once I can tell that Edmund is in a deep sleep, I rush to the satellite phone to call my best friend, completely forgetting that it is midnight where I am, which puts California at about 3 AM with the time zone difference. As soon as she picks up, it clicks with me how late it is.

"Are you joking, Lucas?" she grumbles.

"I am so sorry, Sam. I got so caught up in my excitement I just realized the time there. Should I call back later?"

"I'm up now, jerk," she says. "Might as well tell me what it is that couldn't wait."

Samantha and I have known each other since our undergraduate days. We met at Berkley, both psychology majors. I had an intense crush on her for years, but she had me in the "just friends" category right off the bat. When I finally surrendered the fantasy of one day being more than just a study buddy, we became the best of friends and have been since. She was even in my wedding — luckily our friendship was stronger than the marriage. She is the only person I can think of that has been in my life constantly for more than a decade, other than my immediate family. Because of that, I take no offense to her calling me a jerk when I call her up in the wee hours of the morning. And likewise, she takes no offense to me waking her at 3 AM on a weekday.

"You are not going to believe this," I start. "There are people here!"

"What?" she asks, still half-asleep.

"People!" I repeat. "On the island. There is a little group of six of them and a shaman. It's insane."

"That is insane," she says back. "What are they like?"

"I've only met two so far, but they are both quite intriguing personalities. There is a captain, a man named Sawle, and then this other man, Edmund, who is just a guy like me who was out messing around in the ocean and ended up here. Edmund is actually staying on the yacht with me tonight."

"Lucas, you just met this guy and you're having a slumber party?" Sam asks, disbelieving. "Are you under an island spell or something? That does not sound like the Lucas I know."

"Believe me, I know," I tell her. "You would just have to meet him, though. There's something about him that makes you trust him. It's almost like I've known him in another life or something."

"Sailing makes you so sentimental," Sam jokes.

"Maybe," I say. "But that's not the only interesting tid-bit I have."

"There's more?" Sam teases with mock enthusiasm.

"You could at least feign interest."

"I thought that's what I was doing," she says. "Seriously though, I am interested. This all seems a little crazy. If I didn't know you better I'd think you were on some psychedelics."

"High on life!" I say in an excited whisper. That's the sort of cliché I usually scoff at, but somehow it slipped right out of me.

"Oh, Lucas, please," Sam groans. Sam and I are generally on the same page in our intolerance for gushing sentimentality, so I imagine my zeal is a little obnoxious to her, especially at 3 AM.

Ignoring her annoyance, I go on to tell her all about the hut we found with the photos and that man who looked just like Edmund, and also about Sawle. I tell her about how another sailor had the same premonition that I had when I arrived, too. I also explain to her how strange Edmund acted about the dark and how a fog covered the island as the sun set. A recount of the day's events gives me the chills. As I ramble on, I look out at the island, now hardly visible for the fog.

When I finish, Sam finally says, "That's some pretty intense stuff for your first day. And I will demand some kind of proof of it all when you get back here," she adds.

"I took some of the photos," I tell her. "So I'll have your proof, all right."

"I was kidding, but I would love to see whatever you have when you get back," Sam yawns. "And not too long ago you were a skeptic yourself," she adds.

Sam is absolutely right. I am not the kind of man who gets swept away in an island fantasy. I am also not the type to believe in fate or the intangible, but in the one day I have been on Palmyra something has changed. I am still Lucas, but it feels as though there is some kind of subtle transformation taking place. I may just be caught up in the moment, but even that is unlike me. I can't help but wonder what the weeks ahead hold.

"Lucas?" Sam breaks my thoughts. "Are you there?"

"Sorry about that," I apologize. "I was just thinking. Anyway, I plan to get more," I tell Sam as I hear Edmund stirring in the bedroom. "Hey, I better go now. I think my houseguest might be waking up."

"Be safe, Lucas," Sam tells me. "And be sure to keep in contact. I know these people seem great, but don't let your sentiment blind you, okay?"

"Of course," I assure her. "What is it about psychologists that we are all so leery of others?"

"Because we know others so well," she answers. "Sleep well," she adds with another yawn.

"You, too. Goodnight."

I hang up and sit quietly to see if Edmund will appear. After a few minutes of silence, I decide he must've just been talking in his sleep or rearranging himself in bed. I turn out the lights and hit the hay myself; Blue laying alongside me. It has been a long day, and I am sure tomorrow will be just as exciting. As I drift off, I wonder what the others will be like. Just before I fall asleep, I think of the fog on the island.

ZZZZZ

"Sun's up!"

Edmund's voice breaks into a dream I am having about Blue being swept up in a cloud of fog and taken away over the ocean. His voice overpowers my screams in my nightmare. When I open my eyes, I feel more exhausted than when I went to bed. The nightmare really drained me.

I blink in the sunlight that is coming in from the galley window and reach down to make sure that Blue is still there beside me, next to the couch. I feel his coarse hair and his rough tongue on my hand. I sigh and relax into my pillow for a moment.

"I figured you for an early riser," I say as I finally pick myself up from the couch. "What's on the agenda today?"

"I figured we could try to meet up with the others," Edmund suggests. "I want you to meet the whole crew since we didn't yesterday."

"I like the sound of that," I reply, "but not until I have a cup of coffee."

"Sure," Edmund agrees. "I'll take one, too. But I do think we should hurry. I'd like to get there before everyone is out and about on the island. Don't want to miss them again, you know."

"I couldn't agree more," I say as I get the coffee going and feed Blue.

Edmund and I have our coffee, and get the dinghy ready to go ashore. The three of us load up and head back to the island. Once there, Edmund hits the ground running and we are off to the retreat he showed me the day before. This time, everyone is there. For some reason, even though I had prepared myself, I feel a little overwhelmed to meet everyone at once.

"Well, there he is," says an older woman with ash gray hair and eyes so bright you'd think they belonged to a teenager. "You know, it is nice to check in if you're going to stay out all night, young man."

"I'm sorry, Klara," Edmund apologizes sheepishly. "I was with my new friend here, Lucas, and we decided to stay on his boat for the night."

"Well, you're off the hook because Mr. Sawle told us that we had a visitor. We figured that you were with him." At that, Klara turns to me. "And you must be Lucas." She puts her arms out to hug me.

"I suppose I am." I walk awkwardly into the hug. I didn't grow up in a family so free with their affections, so I feel a little strange embracing a stranger. Edmund was right; she feels like my own grandmother as soon as she wraps her beefy arms around me. She actually feels more like a grandmother than my own grandma, brawny arms and all.

Klara is a good-sized woman, with sun-kissed skin and glowing blue eyes that make her look younger than she is. She is thick, but by no means overweight. She is the picture of health and balance. She has muscle tone that you rarely see in a woman her age, which I imagine comes from vigorous hiking and a 100 percent organic diet. Her long gray hair is tied back in a braid that goes to the middle of her back. Her clothes are light and flowing so that she looks almost like an angel when the sun is at her back. She has a confidence about her, yet is humble. She is welcoming and warm; and I feel comfortable with her already.

Being with Klara makes me feel something that I can't remember ever feeling before. It is the way I imagine a soldier feels when he is reunited with his family after a war or the way the prodigal son must have felt when his father welcomed him with open arms. I feel connected to her, and that makes me feel connected to everything else. I don't know what it is about these people, but they all have that irresistible inner glow that draws me to them.

Klara takes over and introduces me to the others, Dr. Gerrit Judd and the couple, Kalama Wilkinson and her husband, Johnson. Dr. Judd is medium height with a slender, but athletic, frame. He looks to be a little older than Edmund and I, maybe in his early forties. His hair is rust-colored with flecks of gray and he has the kind of skin that freckles rather than tans, so he is the only one on the island who isn't bronzed. He wears a bowler-style hat and a white button-down shirt with a pair of khaki trousers. He looks almost overdressed for the occasion, but I imagine he wears the clothing to keep his fair skin from burning to a crisp in the island sun. Dr. Judd and I shake hands and exchange friendly greetings. Then I turn to the Wilkinsons.

Kalama and Johnson are a beautiful couple in their early thirties. She is petite with auburn-brunette hair that she has tied back in a messy bun. Her eyes are large and gray-blue, and they are by far the most prominent feature of her delicate face. They shine bright against her golden skin, which is lightly freckled across the bridge of her nose. The freckles only seem to make her more lovely and youthful.

Kalama's husband, Johnson, is just as fetching. Unlike his wife he is tall and has an imposing build. He is well over six feet and looks to be at the peak of physical condition. He reminds me a little of Johnny Weissmuller in the old Tarzan flicks I used to watch with my father. He has deep, brown eyes that are framed with slight wrinkles, just enough to make him look distinguished without seeming tired. His hair is so brown it is almost black and it curls at the tips so that its slight unruliness gives him an adventurous and unpretentious air. He looks made for this island somehow.

"I hear you've travelled some ways to visit us," says Johnson as he reaches out to shake my hand.

"A worthy expedition," I respond with a smile as my hand greets his.

Kalama seems to be immersed in some sort of art project made of twigs and leaves, so barely notices my arrival.

"Honey, aren't you going to introduce yourself?" says Johnson, as he places his hand on her shoulder.

I can feel the tension between the two of them. It is obvious by looking at them that they belong to one another, but there still seems to be something muddled between them. They might be Romeo and Juliet in another time, but here and now they are just a struggling couple desperate to work out their differences; trying to hang onto the things that made them fall in love. I know that is a lot to infer upon our first meeting, but sizing people up at a glance is something I do without even realizing it. And besides, I can't help but recall what Edmund told me about how they bicker nonstop, so that tidbit worked its way into my initial observation.

As I look at Kalama and Johnson, I think of all the other couples I have met over the years. I also think of my own failed marriage. I see in them the same promise and doom that I saw in all those other relationships, my own included.

A mix of emotions swirls in my guts as I gaze at the couple. I feel hopeful, heartbroken, scared and happy for them all at once. But as I stand there with them, the negative thoughts begin to fade and feelings of great promise flourish.

I hear a faint whisper in my ear, and soon realize it's Klara that has snuck up on me.

"They have not yet learnt the law of balance, Lucas. In their own time, they will let go of the struggle between light and dark, for both are important teachers. Light from the sun gives us warmth and life. Darkness, on the other hand, brings fear; as it hides what is ahead. When they finally embrace the beauty of both, the energy between them will harmonize. They have simply forgotten balance, and have let the dark eclipse the light."

"What is the light and what is the dark?" I ask, trying to understand.

"Light is love, and darkness is fear," Klara responds. "Both are real."

"What are they afraid of?" I ask, not realizing Klara had walked away to get a drink of water.

I suddenly feel the way the Pentecostals must feel when they begin speaking in tongues on Sunday mornings. I feel like I've been granted special wisdom by a Sage. At this moment in time, the world makes complete sense to me.

8

Once I settle down from my epiphany and get myself refocused, I engage in the goings-on around me. The last thing I want to do is seem disinterested, or appear to not be listening to what the others have to say. I tune back in to the conversation that has been going on without me for the last little while; it doesn't appear that I've missed a beat. Catching the tail end of the dialogue between the Wilkinsons and Klara, it sounds as though all I missed was a discussion on where the doctor and the couple were going to fish for the day.

"I don't know why we always have to go to the same place," I hear Kalama complain.

"You know, dear, you're always full of complaints but never suggestions," her husband replies.

"We'll just let Kalama decide this time then," Klara suggests.

"I suppose the regular place is fine," Kalama sighs.

It's odd, but I feel invigorated by everything around me: the people, the island, the air — everything. The group is welcoming and not one of them gives me a bad feeling, which is a massive relief to me. It makes me chuckle to think how unnerved I was by my first encounter with Edmund just the day before.

Blue sticks by me for the most part, but I can see he doesn't feel threatened in the least by anyone. I am again surprised that he doesn't give everyone a good working over with his nose, but I imagine he is still coming to terms with his surroundings. He must just be giving our new friends the benefit of the doubt without the usual sniffs. I'm glad for this, as it can be uncomfortable for others and me when Blue gets too familiar with his nose.

"Well I hate to meet you and run," Dr. Judd says once the group has decided where they are going to fish, "but the Wilkinsons and I were just about to head out for the day. You are welcome to join us, though."

"Actually, I thought I'd take him to the east end of the island," Klara answers before I can even clear my throat to speak. She turns to me. "I hope I'm not being too forward, I just think there is something on the east end you'd love to see."

"Of course," I say. "Maybe tomorrow," I suggest as I face Dr. Judd.

"Absolutely," he assures me. "And we can get to know one another when we all return this afternoon."

"That sounds fantastic," I smile. "Until then."

"Well then, Lucas," Klara says once the others are walking away from us. "I guess we'll be on our way too."

"I'm ready when you are," I tell her. "Are you coming, Edmund?" I turn to my friend and ask.

"You all go on without me," he answers. "I think I'll do some writing while you go out exploring."

"You're sure?" I ask.

"Indeed," he insists. "You're probably tired of me by now, anyway. Klara will take good care of you," he says, then waves his hands, shooing us along.

"Okay then," I say. "We will see you when we get back. Happy writing."

With that, Edmund disappears into one of the huts. I find myself wondering what he might write about. I wonder if he'll write anything about me, and if he does, what he'll say. In the short time we've known one another, Edmund and I have developed quite a bond. I trust that if he does write anything, it will be good.

As I think of all the things Edmund may have to say about me, it occurs to me that I have never felt so certain about where I stand with someone. With the exception of Sam—and it took me half a decade to feel secure in our friendship—I have never felt that I really knew someone or that they knew me. How strange.

Why do you feel so certain of your friendship with this man you didn't even know twenty-four hours ago, Lucas? As I search for an answer, Klara speaks.

"You and Edmund seem to get along well."

"We really do," I tell her as I fall into step beside her on the path. "I was actually just thinking of that. I know it probably seems silly since we hardly know one another, but I get that best-friends kind of vibe with him."

"I don't think that's silly at all," Klara replies as she looks ahead. "I think it's beautiful. When it comes to forming relationships with others, you have to be a risk-taker. We invest in relationships without guarantees. That is what you're doing with Edmund."

"I am."

Klara's words resonate in me and I think about how right she is. I have only known Edmund for less than a full day, but still I have held nothing back.

Though I keep myself guarded with everyone else I know — even Sam to some extent — I have not been hiding behind any kind of safety wall with Edmund. Instead, I stepped out in front of it and completely exposed my vulnerabilities and life struggles in a way I never do. I have put myself in a place where there's a probability of pain, but there is also a possibility for a real and lasting friendship. It's apparent to me that the reason I have never had true friends or lasting love affairs is because I never allow myself to be that honest with others. Hardly anyone does anymore.

"You're allowing yourself to love and be loved," Klara announces over my thoughts. "That's vital to happiness in life."

"I think I'm learning that right now," I tell her.

"Then I am glad you came here," Klara smiles. "And I am also glad that you came with me today, because what I'm about to show you will work wonderfully into the things you are learning."

"You still haven't said where we're going," I inform her.

"To the field of butterflies," she answers. "To get there, we must go east of the atoll to a place called Barren Island. Did you and Edmund go there yesterday?"

"We might have," I tell her. "We did go to the east part of the lagoon."

"Did you go on foot only?"

"Yeah," I state.

"Then you didn't go to Barren Island. There is only one way to get to it, and it isn't by foot."

"I see," I murmur. "How do we get there then?"

"We have to use a canoe to cross the lagoon. You most likely went as far as Papala or Eastern Island. We'll be going much further than that today."

"I guess I didn't realize it went out further east," I tell her. "I should have researched the island a bit better."

"You'll know everything about it before you leave," Klara says with a grin. "Today you will see things that your mind will not forget."

"You're really building it up," I joke. "I hope that this Barren Island lives up to the hype."

"I think it will," Klara answers thoughtfully. "The lagoon is teeming with fish that come in colors you've never seen. We must be mindful though, as there are also sharks in the lagoon that protect these sacred islets."

"Edmund mentioned that," I say as I shudder. I call Blue to me, just as I had the day before.

"The trip is worth it," Klara encourages me. "And there is nothing to be afraid of, anyway. The sharks won't hurt us."

"What makes you so confident that the sharks won't do anything?" I ask.

"Because I trust they won't," she states very matter-of-factly. "They are simply there to protect their home. We come to observe the butterflies with a loving heart and the sharks know that."

"You really believe that?" I ask. The skeptic in me takes over.

"It's not a matter of belief. I *know* it," she says firmly. "I've been here for longer than I can even remember anymore and I have never once been bothered by them."

"Has anyone?"

"Oh, yes," Klara sighs. "But they weren't here with good intentions. That's why the sharks attacked. There have been some vicious attacks — fatal even — but only on those who came with something wicked in their hearts."

"What happened?" I ask nervously. "What did they want?"

"Well... Palmyra has remained untouched for more than 20,000 years. Even the Polynesian navigators left this coral haven alone to rest silently in the sea. But shortly after the atoll was discovered by the New World, they found the islets were rich in guano and planned to mine the fertilizer to bring back to America." Klara says with a sense of sadness.

"Did they mine the island?"

"No, no guano was ever mined. They never got the chance."

"When Edmund told me about the sharks I had a terrible image of Blue being torn to shreds by thousands of razor-sharp teeth."

"Let go of those thoughts, Lucas. They aren't real. And they aren't worth your time."

"I'll try," I tell her as I keep a close eye on Blue.

"Although you can forget about the sharks, there is something that can hurt you in the water," Klara points out the canoe, tucked away under some fronds on Portsmouth Point.

"What is that?" I ask as we make our way to the canoe.

"The fish," she tells me. "They are beautiful, but many of them are poisonous so you need to be careful about which ones you eat."

"Any tips on which are edible?"

"Steer clear of anything with red. Everything else is okay."

"Red, warning. Easy enough," I say as we drag out the canoe.

"Just be careful because some of them change color at certain times of the day so you won't know."

"I may just leave the fishing to you all," I say, smiling.

"That will work," Klara agrees as we hop into the canoe. "And we're off!" she announces as I whistle for Blue.

I keep my eyes on the water as we paddle through the lagoon. At one point, I dip my hand into the water. It is cool and refreshing. I let my hand stay in the water for a few moments, skimming the surface and making a tiny wake as we travel. I think of the sharks and pull it back in. Every time I see a shadow glide beneath us, I imagine Jaws bursting out of the water and slamming into our tiny canoe. I know Klara said the sharks weren't out for us, but I can't help but shudder when I think of all those teeth and what they could do if they got a hold of a person, or a dog.

"They're not going to hurt you," Klara reminds me. "It's not easy to enjoy life when you're worried. Now surrender your thoughts and enjoy the ride."

I breathe in deep and try to take her word for it. The air is clean and salty, the wind warm, but not sticky or hot. Blue sits between Klara and me with his tongue hanging from his mouth. It looks as though he is smiling.

"Blue seems to believe you," I chuckle.

"He's a good dog. He's wise," Klara grins.

The water is clear as crystal, blemished only by the shadow of the canoe. Violet and bright yellow coral carpets the lagoon floor just like garden moss blankets an enchanted garden. Schools of neon fish weave around beneath us as we glide across the water. I notice many have splashes of red. I take a moment to thank nature for giving us some kind of sign, to let us know which fish might harm us. *I feel at one with the world as gratitude wells inside me.*

We make it to Barren Island in no more than fifteen minutes. Close to shore, I hop out once we're about four feet deep. Klara and Blue hop out a little further in and we pull the canoe to the shore. Off in the distance, just beyond a rock outcropping is an untouched Pisonia forest. Klara points to our destination.

"Some of these trees are over 400 years old," she informs me as we enter the forest. "Unlike the coconut trees, which were brought here by people, these are natives. They thrive here."

In the middle of the forest, I lean up against the trunk of one of the ancient trees. As my back presses into the bark, I can feel the enormous tree's energy. It's as though I can sense its life-force breathing through me. My heart responds as my bare skin comes into contact with the smooth, cool surface of the bark. I feel drugged; I'm intoxicated by the feel of the bark and the earthy smell of the leaves.

Off to the left, I notice a butterfly entangled in a spider's web. My eyes are fixed on the struggling butterfly. For all the beauty that surrounds me, it's all I can see now; that one butterfly on the brink of disaster. I want to save it.

"It isn't your job," she says as I take a step toward the butterfly. "Everything is in perfect balance. We must be close now."

We continue walking and come onto an open field of vibrant flowers covering the ground. I cannot tell what kind of flower, but they are nothing like the white flowers I've seen on the floor of the island so far. These flowers almost glow in the late morning sun. They shine brightly against the green that surrounds them.

At first, I wonder why Klara calls this the field of butterflies, but then I see: What I thought were beautiful flowers begun to move and rise up off the ground. It looks as though a garden is taking flight. Thousands upon thousands of butterflies stir in the breeze. All the colors of the rainbow now flutter around me, and as far as my eyes can see. As I observe this wonder I start to feel part of it. I am speechless at the sight. Klara stares out onto the field with glassy eyes. She looks as though she is also experiencing this for the very first time. We are both awestruck.

I am moved by the way Klara can be fully captivated by something she has already experienced so many times before. The glow on her face, her aliveness, makes me think back to the Wilkinsons and then to the couples back in California that were struggling when I left. If only they could experience every kiss like their first—the same way Klara can experience the field of butterflies.

"The butterfly plays many roles in Native American culture, you know." Klara turns to me.

"I think I've heard that," I tell her.

"Some tribes believe that butterflies would carry wishes up to the Great Spirit," she explains as she faces the field again. "Think of all the wishes these carry."

"This is a good place to be if that is true," I say.

"Other tribes believe that the butterflies bring dreams to us while we are sleeping. Mothers would even tie a piece of buckskin with a butterfly embroidered on it into their children's hair to bring them good dreams while they slept."

"I could've used a butterfly last night," I mumble as I think of the dream with the fog and Blue.

"You had a bad dream?" Klara asks.

"I did," I say. "About Blue."

"Well maybe tonight one of these butterflies will bring you better dreams."

"Perhaps they will," I say. "If I just dream of this it will be a beautiful dream."

Klara smiles. "Beauty like this only exists when everything is in harmony you know. This island has been untouched by most. During World War II, people came and eventually brought with them foreign species, like the coconut tree, and rats, but the island has found a way to balance itself out, even with outside forces working against it."

"So it has found a way to overcome adversity in a way. And has stayed true to itself."

"That's right, in a way," Klara replies. "When the island realized it couldn't overcome the intrusion, it understood their presence served a purpose; so it sought harmony. The island didn't overcome or rid itself of the palms or rodents; they're still here. Instead it adapted to the change and learned to live with them. The island knew that what it feared would eventually leave, when the time was right, but until then the coconuts and rats would remain for a reason. And with that, the island went on to flourish — it healed by expanding its forests and flowers. That is why this place stays beautiful."

"So it healed by integrating the changes," I reflect out loud. "And even if they don't go-away or perish, the island is still happy and growing. They're still serving a purpose, that's why they're still here."

"You got it," she says with a smile. "And before you ask... no, we won't always know what that reason is. What I can say, Lucas, is that life is a delicate balance. It's not always about fighting the changing winds, sometimes it's about letting them carry you. Wherever you may land is the adventure you must embrace. But no matter how rough the trade winds may be, the butterflies will always find their way home; no matter how far they're carried."

"You mean that outside influences will never take away their spirit or their purpose?"

"That's right," Klara responds. "What a wonderful way to be. We nurture our spirit by remembering who we are and where we came from. We all have a part to play as guardians of the Earth; we all do. We must nurture and care for this planet and all its beings; what an amazing gift we've been given. Nature will do its part for us, but we must do ours."

I pay close attention to what she is saying and the way she says them. As I listen intently, I begin to really hear her. Not only her words, but what she means and what she feels. It's almost as if she is speaking to my heart and not my ears. I can step right inside her mind and soul and hear her. I'm no longer hearing her voice but her *intentions;* I feel her purity, and her love and passion for life. I realize that I rarely give others that kind of attention — that kind of devotion to what they are saying. I don't think anyone does anymore. I'm beginning to see there is a whole new way of listening. *It is when we listen with our heart that we begin to truly understand.*

I completely get what Klara is saying. I see how badly she wants humanity to emulate this island, and why she wants this. If we could approach life with compassion, even when outside forces work against us, we too could find our balance the way the island has — with ourselves and in our world. We can't avoid or stop the bad stuff from happening, but when they do, we can acknowledge that they have formed part of our experience — and then use our strengths to keep going, and flourish above it.

It isn't about what happens to us in life that shapes us; it's about how we let these things disrupt our balance. It's that slice in-between what happens, and what we do about it, which is our lesson. Like the island, we have to find ways to balance out, even when something threatens us, whether purposefully or inadvertently. Klara also reminded me, that the things we look at change when we change the way we look at them. With love in our heart, we can see the beauty in everything.

I recall a patient I have who has never had a healthy relationship of any kind because of the relationship she has with her mother. Her mother, I imagine, genuinely loves her daughter, but has unintentionally destroyed her spirit. The mother, like so many others before her, has pushed my patient away in her attempts to protect her, keep her safe, and dodge the mistakes she had made when she was younger. In trying to shield her, she has created an anxious and spiteful mess. The daughter doesn't trust herself to make decisions, and she also doesn't trust others. This has created severe isolation.

The daughter is just like the island, and the mother is like the people who brought coconut trees and rats. They didn't want to hurt the island; they simply didn't think at all about what they were doing or their motives. Unlike the island, the daughter couldn't find a way to balance herself. Because of this, her butterflies quit returning when she became as toxic as her mother. When I get back, I will teach her to find her balance again, despite what has been planted to ruin it. I will have to find my own balance first, and I'm beginning to think I can.

"Like a butterfly breaking free of its chrysalis, there is beauty and wonder on the other side," Klara says.

"Thank you," I whisper.

"You are welcome, Lucas," Klara replies, also in a whisper. "We have to go now, though. The dark is moving in."

9

Klara and I return to the canoe with Blue. She has
the same sense of dread in her eyes that Edmund did the night before. She is no longer the confident
old woman I knew a moment ago. I sense her anxiety as
she moves faster and smiles nervously.

"I'm sure Edmund explained the dark," she says as we
paddle across the lagoon.

"Only that I don't want to be caught in it," I explain.
"Would you like to elaborate?"

"Oh, that's about it for now," she replies.

The way she says, "for now," makes me think there is
more to this island than meets the eye. I've found there
is no use pressing for answers on this island when people
are not ready to give them, so I drop the topic for the
time and help Klara paddle back to shore. When we are
back to the atoll, we replace the canoe in its little hiding
spot and hike back to the retreat.

Everyone is there, waiting outside the huts in the main
area. I notice vines draped across the doors of each of the
huts that weren't there before.

"Why the vines?" I ask.

"Just for peace of mind," the captain answers. "They
are woven from leaves and branches of the Miracle Tree.

Call us superstitious, but we just feel like they stave off bad vibes."

"Like lamb's blood for Passover," I suggest.

"Something like that, I guess," Edmund chimes in.

"Are you ready to eat?" Johnson asks changing the subject. "The captain can cook the fish we caught. He's quite a chef," he adds.

"I have a better idea," I say as I walk over to my back-pack. "I'll cook for you!"

"I hope not protein bars," Edmund chuckles.

"Nope," I say as I pull out some canned salmon and canned veggies. "Just give me a pan and I'll get this ready."

I notice a pan already out by the fire pit, so I grab it. It's filthy, as if it hasn't been used in years. I wonder if they just eat everything raw, like that raw vegan crowd back home. I scrub the pan with a bandana I had in my back-pack. I get the grunge off and get a fire going.

"Just relax and let me take care of everything," I say to my hosts.

Everyone settles down at the table in the middle of the retreat and in no time I serve dinner. As we eat, I tell my island friends about our adventure with the butterflies and the magical experience I had.

"I've been looking at life the wrong way this whole time. I could see it in my patients, but it never registered. It never clicked with me. Sure, it's our perception that becomes our experience; but maybe there is also silver at the end of that murky rainbow, if we choose to see it—even in adversity and dark times. It's time to readjust my focus," I say noticing Edmund's intent gaze.

"I think it's time you do, too," Edmund agrees as he puts down his fork. "Life is what we make of it. Even in the dark of night, we still have the moon to light our way. There is good and bad all around us, but how prosperous our path is depends on the one we choose to see."

"I guess so," I reflect again on the butterflies and Klara's speech about balance.

"There's no guessing, Mr. Psychology," Edmund prods. "Life can be that simple. Here you are, away from all the worries of the world, surrounded by a beautiful ocean and wildlife that people pay to see locked up in zoos. What is there to drag you down?"

"There is always pain," I reply. "But I am beginning to see that I gave that too much energy."

"And why do that?" Klara interjects. "Why focus on the pain when there is just as much wonder to give our attention to? Pain will inevitably come from time to time, but when we focus on it and worry about it, we give it more power than it deserves. If we want to stay in balance, we have to learn to balance our thoughts as well."

"I just can't believe it took me so long to see that," I shake my head.

"At least you did realize it though," Edmund says. "Let us feel pain when we have to — it's there for a reason. But don't be consumed by it. If we only get one shot at life, I say pick out everything beautiful that you can."

"I wish it were that easy," I whisper, to myself as much as to the group.

"Only you can make it hard, Lucas," Edmund replies.

"Not just for me, though. I mean for everyone," I clarify. "I just hope I can keep my optimism and get my patients to see things this way."

"Just remind them that though we cannot avoid pain, we can let life — the beauty, adventure and intrigue of life, not pain, be our focus. I don't think that is too difficult. Like now," he continues. "We've all made a new friend. That we will carry with us. I know I will remember this moment, even after you leave to go back to Santa Monica, how great our conversations were. I will always cherish the time I spent getting to know you."

Edmund's words hit home. People's obsession with the darker things in life stand in the way of their happiness; it is an obstacle to overcome. It has definitely been mine. Hardships will always present themselves, but there comes a time to let go of pain, wrap it up, and place it on a shelf. And as a psychologist, I have to learn to let go of my patients' pain also.

Today I realized I need to shift my focus and re-learn how to have fun again. I have been so accustomed to fretting over absolutely everything that I have forgotten how to enjoy life. I couldn't even be in a relationship because I could only fear the end of it. Even in friendships, I sat and waited for things to crumble instead of enjoying the time together. I never thought about how the good never had to end if I just kept those parts with me.

"I think I forgot how to take time to enjoy life. Lots of people have forgotten that. I only had enough time to do what was on my planner or worry about what I needed to do next so I wouldn't fall behind. That made me anxious about everything—it sucked the joy from my life. And when I did try to engage in life, I could only sit and wait for something bad to happen. How can a joyless person too busy to evaluate their own life come to terms with anything?"

"I don't think he can," Klara says gently.

"You're a wise woman, Klara."

"Oh, I don't think so." She blushes as she sloughs off my compliment. "I think I'm just simple enough not to over think things."

Klara's humility makes me smile. I look down at my plate and realize there is nothing left on it. I was so famished that I had managed to inhale my food even while I was chatting.

"Blue will finish up whatever you all don't eat," I announce as I get up to rinse my plate. "And with that, I think I'm ready for some rest," I add.

"I think we all are," Edmund says as he gets up from the table. "It's almost dark anyway, so it's time to get into the huts. You can stay with me, Lucas. We can play a game of Rummy or some chess to wind down a bit if you'd like before we get some shuteye."

"Sounds good to me," I tell him. "After you, sir."

Edmund and I retire to his hut, which is anything but extravagant. There are a couple of cots that have mosquito netting that looks to be as old as the antiques I saw at the Captain's place draped over them. The floors are dirt and the few items of crudely made furniture are covered in layers of dirt and dust. It looks as if Edmund hasn't actually touched anything for decades, but since they spend little time indoors, I guess housekeeping isn't a priority. I figure that the soil cover that blankets the place is just part of island living.

"I apologize for the condition of my living quarters," he says. I blush as I realize that my thoughts must be pretty apparent to him.

"It's rugged," I joke. "I didn't come to an uninhabited island for turn down service and fresh sheets. I came for this," I assure him.

"I don't know if you're just humoring me, but I like that attitude," Edmund smiles as he pulls a wooden chair from under a tiny table that sits between the two cots. "Let's dust off the cobwebs and play a game, shall we?" He sweeps his palm across the dusty chess board that sits on the table.

Edmund must be a very serious chess player. His set isn't just a run-of-the-mill version you can pick up at a five-and-dime. Beneath its coating of filth, the board is made of oak. I can see that it is both sturdy and ornate; the pieces look to be carved from marble.

"They don't make sets like this anymore," I say as I hold a rook in my hand, admiring the weight and crafts-manship of the piece.

"They don't," Edmund agrees. "Now let's get some use out of this one-of-a-kind set."

I have a small lantern I keep in my gear, which I pull out and turn on for some light. Edmund tells me to keep the light low. He doesn't seem to be a fan of any kind of artificial lighting, and that is something else I like about him. He loves everything that nature has to offer, right down to the light. We play a game and both of us droop in our seats as it goes on. When I finally have Edmund in checkmate, we are both relieved to be finished and able to collapse on our cots for a night's sleep. Blue, who's been lying at my feet the entire time, is already chasing rabbits in his dreams by the time I turn off the lantern and settle down onto my cot.

"Until the morning," Edmund says to me just before I doze off.

ZZZZZ

10

Throughout the night I have strange dreams that disrupt my sleep. Just before I wake up, I dream of a faceless stranger chasing me through the jungles of Palmyra. In the dream I am out searching for my loved ones—my parents and sibling and Sam. It's evening and I know that I have to get to them before dark falls, but I don't know where they are. I can hear them calling, but the sounds seem to be coming at me from all directions. Blue is with me at first, but even he disappears. As the sun slowly fades, I feel the dampness of the fog on my skin.

The calls from the jungle become more intense and panicked. I hear Blue whimpering, but his whimpers seem to move away from me, even as I run toward them. I call out to Blue and to my parents and Sam, and I run in all directions, but I cannot seem to get a hold on where they are. Then the calls of my loved ones turn to the calls of my patients—there's the woman who struggles with her mother, and the couple who cannot figure out how to love one another anymore, along with a few others. I know that they need me, but I also know that the dark is coming. I cannot get to them once the sun has disappeared to the other side of the world.

I'm losing light, running hard now and screaming in desperation. I hear someone close by saying my name. The voice grows louder. I feel hands on my shoulders. Startled, I open my eyes.

"Must have been quite a dream you were having," Edmund says. Blinking, I try to get my bearings.

"It was. No field of butterflies last night." I throw my legs over the bed and reach down for Blue. As I scratch Blue's ears and run my hand up and down his back, I decide that I should call Sam soon and also check in with my family. "Funny how dreams can linger once you're awake," I mutter, trying to shake my sense of disquiet.

"I think I'll go out exploring a bit myself today," I tell Edmund as I throw on my clothes.

"Absolutely," Edmund replies. "We'll all be here by evening. If you change your mind and want a guide, my schedule is wide open."

"I appreciate it," I tell him. "But I think Blue and I will go bumping around by ourselves today, now that you and Klara have given me the tour."

After a quick breakfast, I load my pack with everything I'll need for the day so I won't have to return. I have a full day planned. There is something drawing me to the south islets that Edmund mentioned. I know he said they might be dangerous, but I still want to see the whole place, even those areas the others shy away from. Besides, curiosity has gotten the better of me.

Being as vague as I can be, I tell the others that I'll be gone for the day, as Blue and I set off. I'm especially keen on Kaula Island. I know that the shaman resides somewhere in the area, and I'm more than open to a chance encounter. I know it's not likely, it seems the shaman isn't the type to be stumbled upon unless he wants to be. Either way, I know it will be an adventure.

Hiking through the tropical forest, taking in the scenery, I'm struck once more by the canopy of lush green that hangs far above me, so thick it nearly blocks out the sun. It is a sight that kicks something up in me every time I take a moment to stop and look around. Although I have trekked throughout much of the atoll by now, to see it again all alone is a completely new experience. There is no one there to distract me from my surroundings. I am totally silent as I watch some brightly-colored island birds soaring above me. I take in deep breaths and stand completely still, listening to the boobies calling out to one another; seeing the way the sun and shadows push against each other on the forest floor. The longer I watch the more I see light and darkness coexisting, perhaps even playfully dancing together, rather than struggling for control.

The air is so invigorating that it almost makes me feel drunk. It lifts the spirits like a glass of good wine, but instead of leaving a headache in its wake, there is only the feeling of quiet contentment. Blue and I are alone now, and have made it a ways from the camp, but the spirit of the island—the sea, the sun, the ground and air —make it feel as though I am in the company of great friends I have known a lifetime.

There is a closeness I feel with this place and its people that I don't usually get from others. The feeling of intimacy warms me, but also brings sadness to think that I lack this feeling from all but one of my friends. Not wanting to wallow, I let that thought float away on a warm breeze. I continue onward, genuinely open to all the island has to tell me.

At Aviation Island I veer right and attempt to cross the coral passage south. The tide is too high so I have to go back and take the dingy through the lagoon; to avoid another half-day hike around the atoll. In no time, I am at the shore where Betsy is waiting, silent and loyal. I look down at my watch and am baffled to see that it is nearly noon. Now that my head has recovered from the elixir of the island air, I realize my stomach is grumbling. I want to get to Kaula before I eat, so I call for Blue and make my way to the little boat.

As I putt across the lagoon and past Betsy, I gaze down into the deep, green-blue waters and think. Thoughts of what Klara told me yesterday embrace me, about how the sharks won't hurt anyone with a good heart. I look up at Blue and smile. If anyone in the world has a better heart than his, I'd like to meet him. I watch Blue's tail wag crazily as he waits for us to hit the shore again so he can explore.

When I finally pull the dinghy ashore, Blue runs in the low tide and paws at the sand to let me know he's happy to be here. I decide my stomach can wait until we've made our way to the heart of the island, and so we take up our hike once more.

There is a bit more sun on Kaula; the interior is a little less jungle-like than back on Cooper, but other than that, it looks and feels much like the rest of the place. After the way Edmund described it, or better, the way he avoided speaking too much about it, I expected a spooky place covered with dying trees and wilting foliage — nothing but the caws and hisses of unseen predators — but that is hardly the case. As far as I can tell, everything seems as peaceful here as on the main land.

Blue and I come up on a shallow creek and I stop to dip my hands and head into the water to cool off before we get going again. Just before I immerse my hands, I notice teams of brightly-colored fish just below the surface of the water. My stomach lets out another grumbling complaint to remind me it's well past noon and I haven't stopped to eat.

I can try my hand at cooking up something fresh from the island! I remember how the others didn't seem to take to my canned dinner.

"Stay out of there, Blue," I call out to my companion as I hunt for something in my bag to catch a fish or two. I packed a lunch for the day, but I throw it aside to find anything I might use to catch a fresh lunch.

"Ah ha!" I exclaim as I pull out an empty tin can that I accidentally packed from my last meal. "This'll do!"

With my tin can ready, I get on my knees and kneel over the edge of the creek. The water is so shallow and the creek so narrow that catching a fish won't be difficult. I wait for a good size team to make its way to where I am perched just above the water. As soon as it does, I move fast, plunging the can into the water and scooping up one of the fish. It's a decent-sized catch, and only half of it fits in the can. I whirl around and drop it on the ground so it can't flop its way back into the creek.

"There's lunch," I tell Blue, who just sits and stares as the fish flails about on the sand.

As I am cleaning the fish, I am suddenly reminded of Klara's warning from the day before — that any red on the fish means it could be poisonous. I examine the fish to see if it has red, but now that I've cleaned it, it's impossible to tell. I rummage threw the fish scales that lay strewn across the soil, looking for any tinge of red that may be on them but see nothing. I sit and stare at the fish, contemplating whether or not I should eat it. I do have a lunch already packed, and, I know it's better to be safe than sorry. I start to throw the fish into the stream, but something stops me. Something tells me the fish is fine, and I need to trust my instincts. The feeling is so intense; it almost feels as though someone is there with me, telling me to eat it.

After a debate with myself on whether or not I should risk it, the voice that tells me it's fine wins over the part of me that says the possible consequences aren't worth it. My stomach is grumbling. I am tired of dried fruit and jerky.

The choice made, I pull the portable stove from my pack and cook up the first fresh meal I've had in sometime, and the fish is delicious. Going against caution got me a decent lunch. My stomach is pleased and so are my taste buds. All is well with the world, until I suddenly find it impossible to discern where I came from and which direction I was heading. Completely disoriented, a thick fog is growing in my mind. My heart thumps hard against my ribs.

I get to my feet and start to put my things away when a strange feeling starts in my stomach and bubbles up to my brain. It's as though someone has locked me inside my own head and set off smokescreens so that I can't see or make sense of anything around me. My stomach turns and my eyes refuse to focus. My skin burns hot and turns ice cold a second later. I have poisoned myself. I have to get back to the dinghy and find help.

I take off in a panic, calling for Blue as I trot through the jungle with no sense of direction. I stop to look around me; nothing looks familiar. I have no idea which way the lagoon is. Vertigo creeps in, stealing over my sense of direction. I can't tell if I am moving forward, backwards or up. I begin to run. I don't know what else to do, so I run. My steps echo in my head, sending waves through my vision.

"Come on, Blue," I call. I run on with no idea where I'm going. My head snaps from side to side as I move, desperately trying to focus. But I can't. My mind goes cloudy and then dives into a mist. As I stagger deeper into the atoll, it felt like the trees knew me. They were whispering to me... *come closer, get nearer.* They felt my presence, and I felt theirs. Then the mist clears and the clouds float away.

My legs and chest burn. I can't take another step. I crumble to the ground and let my pack slide off my shoulders. I gulp in deep breaths, trying to let the fresh air drive out whatever it is that has taken control of my senses. I heave and my stomach clenches so hard that it feels like it's pulling all my other organs into it. I try to stand again and am aghast to see a man standing just feet away from me, a stoic look on his face. He looks to be a hundred years old, with wrinkles in his bronze skin so deep he looks like a melting wax statue, but he is steady on his feet and his eyes are alert.

"Do not be afraid," the old man says. "I'm here to help."

"Help what?" I gasp.

"Help you," he answers and takes a step forward. "I am the shaman. I believe you have heard of me."

"What is happening to me?"

"The fish. You should not have eaten it, but I think you know that. The poison is working in your body now. We have to get it out."

"But something told me I would be fine," I explain to the shaman. "I was just listening to my instincts. My intuition said it was fine."

"You were listening to your desires," the shaman says. "But that is not what is important right now. Right now, it is only important that you come with me."

"I don't know if I can walk anymore," I tell him. "My body and my head..."

"You can make it. Just follow me," the shaman insists. "When your body stops, I will take you the rest of the way."

The shaman offers his hand to me. His clothes are made of leather and his hair is long and white, flowing over his shoulders and down his back. Even in my near-delirium, I think of how hot he must be, wearing animal skins on the tropical island. As I grab his hand, I feel a brief moment of clarity and a bolt of energy course through my body. Once on my feet, the dizziness and nausea return.

"We need to move quickly," he says. "To heal you before it is too late."

II

It doesn't take long for my muscles to seize up. My feet stop moving; my body stops responding to what I am asking of it. I try to take another step forward, and feel the ground come up from under me and slam first into my knees, then my chest and face. I try to call for help, but my throat won't allow the words to come out. The shaman scoops me up and I'm shocked at his strength.

I can feel the poison running its course as the shaman carries me back to his hut. It crawls through my veins, trickling through all my organs. My muscles tighten around my bones and it feels like my body is going to suffocate itself. Terror seizes me, and then euphoria. I look around to be sure that Blue is coming—he can't be left to fend for himself if I don't make it. I can make out the outline of his image. He isn't clear, but I know he is there, right beside me.

I close my eyes and give in to the drowsiness that the burst of fear and adrenaline left in its wake. On the inside of my eyelids I see Betsy and Sam and Blue, wagging his tail. For a brief moment, I see my ex-wife. She's smiling too. I had forgotten how to remember her with a smile. It's nice to see her that way again. I wish I could have remembered that while I was married to her.

"You have to wake up," the shaman demands as he shakes me. "If you fall asleep, you will not be able to fight the Axè'ki. I will not be able to fight the Axè'ki. When that happens, your soul could leave you, and then I cannot help."

The shaman's words rouse me out of my stupor. I open my eyes again and look around. Everything is a blur of earth tones set against a canvas of pale blue. The ground and trees and sky all bleed into one another. I try to find Blue again, but it's no use. My eyes won't focus at all now. I may as well be blind.

"I can't see," I gasp. "I'm dying! I can't see!"

"I will know when you are dying. It isn't here yet, but it is close, so we have to hurry," the shaman answers stoically. "Keep your eyes open and your mind aware. We are almost there."

Fighting the exhaustion that was pulling on my eyelids as we went along, I say a quick prayer. I pray to the universe and to God and to whoever will hear me that the shaman gets me back to his place in time. My body aches and my muscles have turned to mush. Breathing feels as strenuous as lifting a Buick. Although I don't know what an Axè'ki is, I know that it is bad and it's not far from me.

As I attempt a deep breath, I feel the shaman come to a halt and lower me to the floor. We are at his hut. I can't see anything, but I can tell that the light is dim and feel the cool of shade, so I know we are inside. Where my muscles have turned to useless mass and my eyes have failed me, I can still smell and feel everything around me. I can smell the earth floor of the hut and the baking fronds that make the walls and ceiling of the shaman's abode. I can feel the silky smooth fur of the skin the shaman has laid me on and smell that death smell of tanned skin.

The shaman wraps me in several skins and then leaves my side. I can hear him moving around but I can't make out what he's doing. I wish he would do something to stop the pain that is now ripping into the tissue of my body. I wish he would give me something to drink that would suck the poison from my guts. I wonder what he is doing just as the smell of burning tobacco meets my nostrils.

"This is an odd time for a smoke break," I wheeze, half-joking and half-terrified that this man is no more a healer than Blue, who I hope is nearby.

"It's for you," he answers. "The tobacco will help fight the Axè'ki while I wait for an answer for the cure."

The tobacco smells sweet. It reminds me of the smell of my granddad's sitting chair. My granddad was a pipe smoker. Nana nagged him about it until the day his heart gave out. She was afraid he would get cancer or die of a stroke if he didn't stop, plus she hated the smell, she said. I always loved the smell, especially after he passed. His pipe didn't do him in after all, and it left a lingering scent of my granddad for us to hang on to after he was gone. I haven't smelled tobacco for some time. I realize I also haven't visited their graves for far too long.

The shaman begins to chant. He's no longer near me, but I can still smell burning tobacco and he sounds as if he is still in the hut. I can hear his footsteps encircling me; he must be dancing. I cannot understand what he is saying, but the rhythm of his chanting soothes me. I feel the power of the words, even though I cannot understand them.

"Herbs will keep the Axè'ki from killing you," he finally says to me. "It is your body, not your spirit, that needs to be cleansed."

"It was the fish," I tell him. "That is what is doing this."

"Yes," the shaman agrees. "But I have herbs to get the poison out. Now swallow." He lifts my head and puts a cup to my mouth.

I choke down the remedy. It tastes bitter, but leaves a sweet aftertaste. Once I have drunk the entire cup, the shaman continues to blow smoke over my body. In no time, I feel the pain in my stomach eases; my eyes come into focus and my ribs let go of my lungs. I take a deep breathe in without struggling. I can feel my muscles trembling; they are weak, but I can feel them and use them again. I exhale slowly then I sit up and look around me.

The hut is large — much larger than the shelters back at Sky. The walls are made from fronds, dried grass and wood from the Pisonia trees. It's built in a dome shape without corners or edges. The entire place is covered with skins. There are skins on his cot, skins along the walls, skins covering the floor in places. There are buckskins, fox skins, coyote skins, and some skins that I cannot make out. I am cloaked in what looks to be coyote skins. The shaman has two tables each covered with buckskin. On one of them, I can see the feathers of different birds. The other table has jars lined up, filled with what I assume must be herbs. Over his bed hangs a large pouch made of buckskin, but I can't tell what's in it.

"How do you feel?" the shaman asks.

"Much better," I tell him. "Thank you so much. I would have died if you wouldn't have come along."

"Yes, you would have," he agrees.

"You must be quite a hunter," I say, nodding toward the skins.

"Those I acquired when I first became a shaman. I did not hunt them; I received them. I use them to heal—to help keep the Axè'ki away from others."

"You keep saying that word. What is that? The poisonous fish?"

"Axè'ki is pain. It's a spirit, a bad spirit that shoots pain into people. It can be a poisonous fish, or it can be illness, or any other animal. It comes in many forms, but all of them are pain."

"So it is just a word for pain then?"

"It is more than that, but to simplify it, yes; it is a word for sickness."

"You said the fish I ate was Axè'ki."

"Yes it was; Axè'ki can appear in many ways. As a shaman, I can see it, but others can't. It is the reason I became a shaman, because I can see what others cannot. That's not important now. Rest is important. The poison is gone from your body and unable to do harm, but you need rest to get your strength back, so focus on that." He blows tobacco smoke over me one last time.

"Thank you again," I tell him.

"You do not need to thank me. This is my purpose," he says to me as he begins to move me out of the hut. "The fresh air will be good for you."

Outside, there is a fire burning not too far from the hut. I don't recall a fire when we came in, but I was also nearly blind and on the verge of death. The shaman moves me near the fire and takes a seat. He is right—the fresh air is cleansing. I take deep breaths and try to relax so completely that I feel as though I am melting into the ground. Blue is by my side again. He is acting a bit strange in the presence of the shaman, but he is by my side and beginning to settle down. The world feels like it's coming back into balance, along with my body and mind. A strange feeling swells inside me—like the poison somehow refreshed my body. I realize it's not the poison that is making me feel rinsed clean, but the herbs the shaman gave me that passed the poison from me.

In the quiet of the afternoon, as I listen to the pop and sizzle of the fire, I have a revelation. Confronting a toxin and taking steps to remove it has made me feel reborn. Whatever it was that the shaman gave me removed that which was harming me and left me feeling like I never have. The poison was working to destroy me, but when the shaman gave something to neutralize it, the concoction tipped the scales and went straight into overload. My energy rises and I feel more alive than I ever have. Maybe he gave me too much of the good stuff. Although physically exhausted from the experience, it's a different kind of tired—welcome and euphoric.

"Those herbs worked wonders." I turn to the shaman. "I have this indescribable feeling, like I've gotten rid of the heaviness that was holding me down long before I ever ate a poisonous fish. Maybe that's just the little bit of the poison left in me talking."

"It isn't the poison," he answers. "Poison brings pain and confusion. You are feeling the opposite. That is the good medicine. Let yourself feel every bit of it. It is good for the soul."

"I can't tell if it is the contrast to being so close to death or if I am really on the verge of some epiphany; I've never felt anything like this before," I explain.

"That feeling you feel," the shaman replies, "is the way you should live your life."

"I don't know if eating a poisonous fish to get here would be worth it in the long run."

"You won't always need a catastrophe to settle in order to feel real peace." He turns to look me in the eyes. It is the first time he has addressed me in such a direct way. The contact seems almost confrontational, but when I look at him, I can see that there is no aggression. He is just making sure that I hear him.

"Are you a fortune teller as well as a shaman?" I ask. "That wasn't meant to be flippant," I add quickly. "I mean that earnestly; is there something you see in my future, some change for me?"

"I'm as much a fortune teller as you are," her answers. "Let this be your new understanding; there cannot be harmony without being *peace-full* during the tough times. When you have peace on the inside, you will be unchained from your fears. Then you will have true happiness, no matter what happens around you."

"If nothing else, I understand I shouldn't eat anything I catch around the atoll without someone to okay it," I smile.

"You didn't know some fish were poisonous?" he asks.

"No, I did," I reply. "Klara told me, and I even thought of it before I ate the fish, but I felt like something told me it was okay — my intuition or something. I guess my inner voice can't be trusted though."

"It was not your intuition. Good and bad are all around us. When we haven't trained ourselves to hear only the good, the bad can step in and lead us astray. I said it before, it was your desires that you could hear, your earthly ego. Something told you to follow your desire so you would do what was wrong. It's when you live with your heart, and see the magic of life, that you'll hear your soul speak," he tells me. "Enough for now. Close your eyes and get real rest, just for a bit."

I roll to my back and face the skies. I see neon birds floating and tracing their own unique patterns in the powder blue canvas above me. The sun is just barely past its halfway mark, so it must be a little after one. I have plenty of time before the dark comes, so I relax into the coyote skin and close my eyes. I feel totally content right now; life is good. For a second, I almost feel uneasy because the feeling is so foreign. But then I think of what the shaman said about how I should always feel like this. I let this moment exist as if it will never die, and I doze off. Just before I fall into a dream, I wonder if there really is a way to hang on to this feeling. It could be the key to the real contentment that I have been missing for so long.

12

I wake up after what feels like hours of sleep, but I can see the sun hasn't moved much, so I couldn't have been out too long. I lean up and use both my hands to brace myself into a sitting position. Blue is near my feet, his head resting on my shins. The shaman is right where I left him, sitting still and quiet beside the fire, like a monument left to memorialize a tradition that time and skepticism has wiped out.

"How long was I out?" I ask, disrupting the silence that hung heavy between the two of us.

"No more than an hour," he answers. "You slept a deep sleep. That's good."

"I feel better—rested. But I feel like I haven't eaten in days."

"I have tea for you, and some bread. You feel hungry, but you need to go easy. Your body may still be a little upset that you put a poisonous fish in it."

He brings over a cup that looks like it was made from the soil of the ground I am laying on and some bread.

"You're quite the host," I tell the shaman as I take the tea and bread. "And I don't think I've even introduced myself to you. I'm Lucas. I'm here from California, visiting the island."

"Yes, I've heard," he informs me.

"I've heard of you too, but only as the shaman."

"Right, well, hardly anyone ever calls me by my tribal name. Mostly I am just called Shaman."

"Well I am happy to finally meet you, even if I'd rather have done it under different circumstances," I smile weakly and take a sip of my tea and then go on. "So someone told you about me then?"

"No one told me. I heard. I stay quiet, tucked away unless I am needed, but I am nearby more than you know. I hear things. I see things. I know who you are even if you have forgotten; and why you have come," he explains.

"Well, thank you for being there today."

"You don't need to thank me. I..."

"Really, I'd be a goner if it weren't for you," I interrupt. "I can't thank you enough. I just wish I could repay you somehow."

"It is my purpose, it's why I am here," the shaman says again.

"Saving silly tourists from poisonous fish is your purpose in life?" I inquire, trying not to sound glib. The last thing I want to do is offend the man who just saved my life.

"To help anyone who needs me on this island," he answers. "It is what I was meant to do—my meaningful purpose."

"That's pretty noble... to live isolated on an island just so you can help whoever might stumble upon it and get themselves into a jam. Doesn't pay well, I imagine," I tease, trying to get the shaman to smile.

"I am successful in life, not because of the money I make, but because I am doing the thing I was intended to do. I sought and found my calling, I followed it, and I am of service to others. That is all the pay I need," the shaman explains without cracking a smile. My jokes aren't going to fall with him.

"You're one in a million then."

"Perhaps, but I hope not."

"I know people who are doing what they're good at — stuff they love and dreamed of doing, but they all expect to make a decent wage in return. They want to be paid for their skill, you know?"

"The money they make, it's not the measure of success; it's the consequence of it."

"That's very true I guess."

"They make it because they do what they were meant to — they're being what they were meant to be. The way they help others, that is their success. Money is consequential. If it is the focus, success is shallow and incomplete."

"I think most of us are probably a little shallow and incomplete," I say.

"That is why so few will ever truly live their purpose. Their soul is speaking but they fail to hear."

That one struck a cord with me. If I didn't know better, I'd say the shaman is now speaking directly to me.

"I am lucky in a way that my culture remained unmolested by a society that is consumed by materialism and the negative side effects of a long-standing capitalist system."

"I didn't think that anyone could hide from materialism."

"You are from California," he states. "Have you heard of Shasta?"

"Like the mountain?" I ask.

"Like the Indian nation," he corrects me.

"I don't know. Surely I have," I say apologetically, feeling guilty that I haven't heard of this man's people. I may as well have been one of the settlers who arrogantly took his people's land hundreds of years ago.

"We're not a recognized nation by the federal government," he explains. "That is why you may not have heard of my people, but we are there and we exist, whether we are recognized or not."

"It's awful that the government doesn't recognize the nation," I empathize.

"I think they will. My people are warriors and there has been progress made. Like I said, we are still a people and we work to keep our culture alive. As long as we do that, we have a chance."

"And so you became a shaman in your tribe then? Not just out here on the island?"

"I did," he affirms. "I received the calling when I was young. That is how Shasta shamans are chosen; they receive a sign."

"Like a vision?" I interrupt.

"Like a nightmare," he answers. "They usually come during a trance. That is how mine came to me."

"Seems a foreboding way to be called to do what you were meant to do," I suggest.

"It is a good way to learn not to let fear in from the beginning," he tells me. "It may come in the form of a nightmare, but it is a calling and when you have a calling, you must accept it graciously and respectfully, rather than fear it."

"I think that I have been terrified of my own calling at times," I say, thinking aloud.

"You should readjust your thoughts then," the shaman replies. "That fear will hold you back, and it will only bring more fear."

"I don't know," I respond as I stare into the now smoldering fire. "Some say there is nothing wrong with a healthy dose of fear—that it keeps us in line and on our toes—that it keeps us alive."

"That's nonsense," the shaman snaps. "Staying focused keeps us in line and alive. Fear only shows us things we have missed, and often carries poison like that fish you ate."

"Do tell," I say, bemused by this idea that we should and can avoid all fear.

"When I was still in Northern California living with my people, I was chosen to be a shaman. A shaman has power—power to heal and power to see things. Those are good things. But shaman can also be seen as bad. At one time, if a shaman lost too many patients, others began to see him or her as a witch, and that could mean death. Now though, death has been replaced with excommunication, which can feel just as intense."

"I don't want to sound rude or ethnocentric, but so far it sounds like being a shaman is a curse, not a blessing," I interject.

"That could be true. In my culture, the shaman is respected, but not liked. It isn't something that anyone aspires to be because of the taboos and the isolation that comes with it. But I realized that being a shaman can be either the most fulfilling thing I could do, or it could be a burden that I am forced to bear. The difference rests only in my attitude about my calling."

"So you're telling me that an attitude adjustment could make being an outcast that gets nightmares and could have been killed a good thing?"

"Exactly," the shaman replies with a nod.

"I don't get it. I consider myself a pretty intelligent and even insightful individual, and I can't wrap my head around that."

"I was pre-destined to become a healer, which is something that Shasta people do avoid, but I put only positive energy into my calling. I let everything work for the good. I eventually set out and landed here, and it was here I found my meaningful purpose. When our soul speaks, we must listen. It spoke to me, and told me where I must go. When we progress towards a worthy idea, and are of service to the greater good in some way, we are successful — whatever path that may be. So here I am, in my true home, protecting the residents of this island. It is here that I found meaning and my sense of belonging."

"But it could have gotten you killed back home," I argue.

"I made the conscious decision to see my calling as a gift. There is a great force in this universe Lucas, and that force is within each of us guiding our path. We must play our part too — and make worthy decisions for our life. When the path is too wide we may stray and lose our way; we become confused. When the path is too narrow we lose sight of the big picture. But when the path we walk is the right one, it leads us to where we need to be," says the shaman.

"But how do I know if I'm on the right path?"

"You'll know when you're not. Your guide will gently nudge you. And if that doesn't work, you may get a shake," he says with a smile.

The shaman continues, "We create our reality. Think about it Lucas, almost everything in your life was first imagined. We become what we think about most often.

What we focus on expands and becomes our reality, no matter if it is positive or negative. I focused on the good and made that my reality. I have the gift to heal and to save people. I can see Axè'ki, which means I can keep them from hurting others. I can talk to the earth and our Creator and get answers. That is what I put all my energy into."

I dig my heels into the ground and listen closely as the shaman goes on. "Putting our energy on the things that can hold us back acts as the biggest hindrance in our lives. Once we have heard our calling, or made a goal to do what we feel we were destined to do, we will soar. We must keep faith that something greater than us is working with us. When you get to the point of *knowing* our Great Spirit is real, you will no longer have doubt, then you are truly on your way to greatness. That's when we are reminded that we are heading the right way. That means we remain focused, and never let the negative scare us. There is no room for fear when we are living our meaning and serving our purpose."

"I would give anything to live life that way," I tell him.

"We become what we think about," the shaman states as he stares into the fire. "You can be what you want to be, Lucas, but it has to be your focus — and aligned with your souls intention for you."

"I know my purpose is to heal humanity, and to inspire them to live with abundance instead of lack. All I think about is how I want to be better, and help more people — how I want to clear myself of the clutter and be the best I can be."

"This works two ways. Are you thinking about how to reach your success or how you are a failure? Poison grows as easily as weeds."

I sit up and consider all the shaman has told me. It all makes perfect sense, but still I don't know how I can just stop myself from having another toxic thought. I don't know how to stave off self-doubt or fear of failure. The longer I think about it, the clearer it becomes.

The shaman is right; we become what we think about. My beliefs have shaped my reality and how I see life. They have also made me what I am today, career and all. I know my beliefs make me feel the way I do. When I look into the mirror I see the man I should have been, instead of embracing the man I have become. If my failures and fears were a night sky, there would be no daylight. If I can reshape the way I see myself, and realize I am already whole, then maybe things can be different. I don't need to be fixed, I just need to keep growing—maybe that's what the world needs to hear. I know the man in the mirror will never smile first, until I smile at him.

Again, I think of grandpa. I think of how much I loved him and how I never wanted to leave when I was with him. And then one day he disappeared. I was left with nothing but the smell of his smoking chair. That was when I started to shut myself off. It was the first time I experienced real loss—real pain—and I didn't want to feel it again because a smell can never replace the sound of someone's voice or the feel of their arms wrapped around you. A smell can't tell you jokes or slip you sweets when your parents aren't looking. I let a painful experience start running my life at eleven, and it was time to let it go. It was time to hold on to the memories of my granddad, not the memories of losing him. It was time to do that with every experience I had.

"When you see what you can feel, then you see magic everywhere," the shaman says breaking my thoughts. "When I was a healer back in my homeland, I got to see the good I could bring into other people's lives. That was all I needed to keep going. I could remove pain and suffering, and that moved my soul."

"But you knew that you could be kicked out of your community if too many people got too ill to save. Didn't that scare you?"

"That never happened because it wasn't what I thought about," he answers. "You become your thoughts, Lucas. My thoughts were always good. I focused on the moment; I had appreciation and gratitude in my heart. It didn't matter that I may one day be run out of my community or seen as a witch. In the moment, I was helping. My intentions were pure."

"So you were focused on the moment, sort of like the Buddhist mindfulness practice," I say.

"I was, and that allowed me to help so many. And I continue to help here. I found my new place here, and I have been able to heal others on the island. That is what keeps me going now — and why gratitude wells inside me."

"So I'm not the only one who has had a brush with death, then?" I inquire, a little relived that the others have at one time needed help as well.

"Well, maybe not in a physical way," he answers. "But some have needed spiritual saving, and I have been blessed to guide them back to wholeness."

"Spiritual saving? That sounds a little evangelical."

"Everyone has a spirit — not just the fire and brimstone preachers," he says turning away from me. "You may find it a surprise, but Klara was the first I ever helped on this island."

"Klara?" I whisper. "She seems so in touch with everything."

"She is," he says, "now. But that wasn't always the case. When Klara arrived here, she was a bundle of fearful, nervous energy. She was afraid of this island, of her future, of herself. Today, you needed physical healing, but she needed spiritual healing, and that is what I did."

"How?"

"That's not for me to share, but suffice it to say, she has become a new person. The beautiful person she was meant to be — that she always was, but that fear kept trapped inside her."

"So that is why she is so in tune with everything now," I mutter to myself, reflecting on what the shaman has said.

"She learned to love herself and others with her heart. That is a key to true contentment — to get lost in that which inspires us and uplifts our spirit. Seek out good conversations, healthy relationships, nourishing food, activities that make you feel good."

"That sounds almost hedonistic," I suggest.

"Life will always find a way to balance itself out, I can assure you of that. There is no need to seek the bad. Your part is to seek the good and follow your happiness. Life is to be enjoyed; and your joy becomes a gift to serve others. I heard you say you are a psychologist, yes?" he turns to me and asks.

"Yes. You are lurking around, aren't you?" I reply, trying to remember when I said that and figure out where the shaman was hiding to have heard me say it.

"Do you enjoy your work?"

"Mostly," I say. "It used to be what got me out of bed in the morning. It still does in a way. The spark is still there but it needs rekindling."

"Think back. Why was it you loved it so much?"

"I saw the change I was making. I knew I was making changes in people, changes that would affect their lives in an enriching way," I answer. In that moment, the fog lifts and I see precisely what the shaman means. "My joy, my passion, my success — it all centered on how well I served others. I was a success when others found their own path in life."

"Aha!" The shaman smiles for the first time. "Although many can't see it and would debate this, overall people are still good. We get tainted by bad experiences and hurt, but we are all born with pure hearts. Our motives may sometimes become skewed as we age, but most of us want to do what is good. If we can get into touch with the goodness that is there and let the Great Spirit guide us always, then we begin to see real success."

"So walking in the Light where it feels good, isn't such a selfish thing after all."

"That's right," he responds, "provided our intentions are pure — we must not be harming others along the way. It is not selfish to chase after pleasure, Lucas. Allowing ourselves to enjoy life makes us happy people. When we are happy, we stay focused on what's important and do our best to serve others. When we let go of our stories of hurt and pain, we open up to enjoying the good life. When we can do that, we are able to lead others to happiness as well, and that is an amazing thing."

"Like when Klara took me to the field of butterflies," I say. "She was sharing her happiness."

"Yes," he nodded. "And you lived in that one beautiful moment, and that beautiful moment will replace a bad one."

"So we shouldn't feel petty for chasing joy. We should embrace it and share it."

"As long as we are sharing our gifts—whether it is something we know well and pass down to all of humanity, or something that we can do to let others feel content—then we are not living selfishly. Keeping our gifts locked away and buried inside us, that is petty."

"How do I get back the joy I once had for my craft then?" I ask.

"Reconnect with your reasons and the greater purpose that guided you to it. Embrace the changes you're helping create in your patients and on the earth. Refocus on the beauty you're manifesting, and nothing else. Do not let distractions sway you."

I suppose it is just my cynical nature trying to keep its grip on me, but as the shaman talks about focusing on that which is positive, I remember the one glaring negative about the island—the darkness. If anyone could finally explain it to me, it would be him, so I abruptly change the subject. "What is in the darkness that people are so afraid of?"

"These are things we do not speak of," the shaman replies, avoiding a straightforward answer. "What we focus on expands—good or bad. We must dwell on the Light that surrounds us and all that is good."

I press him for answers. I want to know, once and for all, what I am running from. I want to know why we have to avoid the darkness and why everyone shies away from the topic whenever it is mentioned. It makes no sense to me. This island is full of amazing people—adventurers who fear nothing, people who set out into the great unknown and have taken up residence on an island cut off from the rest of the world. How can these people be scared of the dark?

The shaman mentions again that he protects the island and the residents, that he's here to keep us from harm, and that the voices I heard coaxing me to eat the fish are part of the darkness that everyone is so careful to avoid. They are felt strongest on the southern islets, including Kaula Island where we are currently. He tells me when our spirit is weak and mind is not clear that we are more susceptible to its dark influence. He explains to me that they also descend upon Palmyra after nightfall, but cannot cross water or touch anyone who is on the water, which explains why Edmund opted to stay on Betsy the first night we met.

"When we hold firm to our virtues and live from the heart, we have strength greater than the darkness around us," the shaman says.

"Okay, but what is it that is out there? Who are they and what do they want?"

"According to some of the natives of Papua New Guinea, the Great Spirit who lives high above the clouds created the earth and everything on it. He divided the world into several levels. After death, spirit people can travel from one world to another. The time on Palmyra is split into days, and days into two halves, from sunrise to sunset —the day is for the living; and the other is time for the spirits. Most spirits are not to be feared; we learn to co-exist, but it is best to acknowledge that night is for them, and day is for us. This place is theirs as much as ours."

"But who are they? What do they want? And why are we running from them?" I push.

"You've had a full day, Lucas, and now the day is coming to an end. You and your partner there had better get back to camp before the others start to worry. I'll take you back most of the way," he says, ignoring my question. "And in the future, be sure to stick to fish the others have caught..."

13

"I think it's time for you to go now," the shaman says, looking at the sun, which is hanging low in the sky now. "I'll walk with you to your boat."

The shaman is quiet as we walk. The silence makes it so that I can hear the bottoms of my feet hit the ground. Blue stays on the side of the shaman. He must really trust him.

"This is for you," he says, holding out a wooden figure. "It is a totem for you."

"This is a panther, isn't it?" I ask examining the totem.

"It is. It will keep you safe the rest of the way."

"That is very kind of..."

"You should go now," the shaman insists, putting his hands on my shoulders and turning me toward my dinghy.

"You're right. Until we meet again then?"

"Yes, until we meet again," the shaman agrees.

The lagoon is eerie now that the sun is sinking into the ocean. A school of red fish passes beneath Blue and me. It reminds me that one little fish nearly sent me to the spirit world. Life is so fragile, and at this moment mine also feels very empty. I feel so insignificant. Even with Blue beside me, loneliness envelops me as I putt across the lagoon. Had I died today, Sam might realize something went awry in a week or so. Other than that, my death would go unnoticed. A knot suddenly forms in my throat. No one knows where I am. If the shaman wouldn't have found me, I would have died and a select few would miss me. My eyes burn and blur and my limbs feel like they've been replaced with water hoses. Sadness is overwhelming.

I felt like this once when I was a child. I was twelve then. It started with ennui. Next I felt depressed. Finally I was consumed with the feeling that I was destined to feel awful forever. I was stuck, being sad and pathetic. When it got to be too much, I told my sister that I didn't want to live anymore.

"Don't even say something like that, Luke," she said, her eyes glossed with tears and bulging.

"It's just too hard, you know?" I cried. "Everything is too hard. Mom and dad are gone, and..."

"I'm here," she interrupted me. "You can't just leave me. You can't. I need you."

"No you don't," I sniffed.

"I do. I always will... I... Remember when you stole that grocery bag from the neighbor down the street?"

"Yeah," I mumbled.

"And the police came to the house. What did I do?"

"I dunno."

"I know you do. Tell me, Luke. What did I do?"

"You said I was with you all afternoon."

"I did say that, because you're my partner in crime. We're both in this together and we'll always look out for each other. Do you hear me, Luke?"

"Yeah," I said to the ground.

"Lucas," Leah said firmly. "I mean that. It's me and you now. It's me and you always. I need you. Really, I do."

I haven't talked to my sister in at least three months. I hardly remember to send her a card on her birthday. Some years a week would pass before I had realized that I missed her birthday altogether. How do you forget the birthday of someone who saves your life? How do you go months not speaking to your partner in crime?

A shadow drifting on one of the south islets, not far from Paradise Island, glides into my periphery and interrupts my sad recollections. Nothing could make a shadow like that. I turn and squint in the direction of the silhouette I swore I just saw. Nothing is there. My eyes must be playing tricks on me.

The sun is almost completely submerged into the blue waters of the ocean now. The island is getting dim. Grays cover the ground now that the light of the sun is gone. Grays start to cover everything. The settling darkness doesn't sit well with me. A boulder weighs heavy in my abdomen as I think of all the things the others have said about the night. The smell of the lagoon and the earth overwhelms me. My senses are in overdrive.

The closer I get to land, the more shadows I notice. I can't make out their origin, but I see several shadows cast on the shore that I'm about to step foot on. These are the shadows the others have talked about. This is why I need to be back at camp with the others. My heart pounds and my breath quickens. I have to get to Sky. I grab for Blue's collar to keep him close to me. I hear the shaman say, "Let go of fear, Lucas, and they'll go away."

"How'd you get here?" I turn toward the voice. There is no shaman. "Hello?"

I turn to see where he is as a swarm of neon butterflies lifts up from the middle of the lagoon right beside my dinghy. Klara's face flashes in my mind. I can almost feel her sitting beside me, petting Blue as I grip his collar. I let go of the collar, take a breath, and the pounding in my ears subsides.

"See those butterflies? Those mean we're going to be fine, Blue," I say, my eyes fixed on the brightly colored cloud that is lifting to the heavens.

The butterflies scatter and disappear. I realize that I am still on the water—on the water I am safe. I dig my hand down into my pocket and pull out the wooden panther. Just feeling the smoothness of the wood against my palm eases my anxieties. I pull the totem out and rub my thumb along the carved figure. The points of the ears tickle the tip of my thumb. I study the details of the panther's face and feel comforted. Tracing the eyes and the nose with my pointer finger, I feel safe.

"Thanks," I say to the shaman, wherever he may be.

Blue snuggles up to my feet in the small dinghy. He lets out a sigh, laying his head on my left shoe. I look to the shore and then back to Betsy. I look down at Blue, who has had quite a day himself.

"You think we should stay on Betsy tonight, just the two of us?" His bushy tail wiggles in reply. "The catamaran it is then. We'd have a long walk back to camp, wouldn't we? I need some time alone anyway."

ZZZZZ

"I'm starved, Blue. How 'bout you?"

Blue is already sitting in front of his dish, so I know the answer to that. I give him a can of dog food and get to my own dinner. With some food in me to take my mind off my grumbling stomach, I realize how filthy I am. After a cool refreshing shower I get ready for bed.

The dryer buzzes while I'm brushing my teeth. *I'll fold the clothes when I finish my routine.*

The washer and dryer are in the bathroom that is right off the master bedroom. The smell of the fresh, clean clothes is comforting. I breathe in deeply and see home for a second. I miss it. I miss the feel of home, even though I love the catamaran, and I am by no means toughing it. The rooms are spacious and well-decorated. My bedroom on the boat may be more luxurious than my bedroom at home, with cashmere throw rugs and bedding that feels the way heaven must. But there's just something about home, even for an adventurer. Sam pops into my head as I take the warm clothes from the dryer and sprawl them across my bed. There are several cushions, real merino cushions, she got me as a boat warming present, on the single-seat lounge chair next to the clothes. She knows how much I love soft fabrics. I remember the day she gave them to me and smile.

Reaching my hand into the pocket of a pair of shorts I feel something. It's a wadded piece of paper—maybe something I gathered from my voyage the day before. The crumpled paper brings back the memory of the pictures from the shack—the ones I slipped into my pack. I drop the shorts and abandon folding laundry.

"Where'd I put my pack, Blue?" I ask as I search the cabin. "Ah, here it is. Right where I left it."

Sifting through the supplies, my fingers finally feel what it is I am looking for—the photo. I slip it out and collapse onto the lounger behind me. As I study the images in the photo, I can see clearly that the young man is Edmund. It must be. I feel the hair stand up on the back of my neck. The people with Edmund look familiar too.

They are Dr. Judd, Klara and Captain Sawle. Edmund is so young though. It makes no sense.

Turning the photo over I can see faded writing that is mostly illegible. There is definitely an "18" written, however. It looks to be a date. The last two numbers are unintelligible, but it has to be a date. *What is going on?*

A high-pitched alarm goes off in the cabin of the boat that nearly causes me to choke on my own heart. It's the satellite phone. Sam must be calling. No one else has the number. If they do, they don't know to call it, anyway.

"I've been trying to reach you," Sam blurts, seemingly agitated. "I had this horrible feeling that something happened to you. Are you OK?"

"That's so strange. You must have a sixth sense about me because..."

"Because what? Are you okay?"

"Calm down, Sam. Yes, I'm okay. If I weren't I probably wouldn't be talking to you, right?"

"Okay, whatever," she snaps. "So what is going on?"

"Well I almost did myself in is all."

"What? How?"

"It was stupid, really. I ate a poisonous fish I guess, but this..."

"You did what, Lucas? How do you..."

"Sam, please. Can I get through this?"

"I'm sorry. It's just this feeling I've had and this poisonous fish story. It's got me on edge I guess."

"It's fine, but can I get through my story now?"

"Yes," she sighs.

"So I ate this fish that ended up being poisonous, but the shaman on the atoll happened upon me and I guess he gave me an antidote. I thought it was just good luck he found me, but then I got back here."

"And?"

"And I'm looking at this picture I took from an abandoned little shack and I swear the people in the photo are all the people here on the island."

"Why is that weird, Lucas? So they took a picture together?"

"It's not that they are in a photo together. It's that the photo looks to be old, very old. And Edmund looks much younger than the others, but he isn't. It just makes no..."

"It's probably just beaten up because it's been in a shack, Lucas."

"Maybe, but..."

As I'm talking to Samantha I notice something I hadn't about Edmund yet. Looking closely at the young Edmund in the photo I see that he is holding a scroll in his hand. A scroll just like the one the captain was writing on! I am in the twilight zone.

"Are you there still?"

"Yeah," I whisper back absently.

"Well anyway, I was calling to make sure that everything is okay out there. I can't say why, but I just have this feeling you shouldn't be there," she says with a graveness in her voice I'm not accustomed to. "There's something not quite right on Palmyra."

There is some splashing in the water outside of the boat that keeps me from answering Sam. Blue lifts his head and his hair bristles. A guttural growl escapes him. The splashing seems to be getting closer to us.

"Ahoy there!" a voice calls from the lagoon.

"Hold on, Sam."

"Wait, what is happening, Lucas? What is..."

I drop the receiver so I can get a good look out of the window. Squinting into the darkness I see a boat drifting atop the water. I see the oars moving up and down, breaking the surface of the water as they plunge in to move the boat forward, toward me. As the boat gets closer I see that it is Edmund. He isn't alone. Kalama and Johnson accompany him. I slide the photo into a nearby drawer and pick up the receiver again.

"It's just some of my friends from the island. They're coming to visit" I tell Samantha.

"I'll call you in a couple days, then" Samantha says. "Be safe, Lucas."

"Sure," I promise.

"What are you doing here?" I call out to the dark lagoon.

"We wanted to make sure you're alright," Edmund answers. "We haven't seen you most the day."

"But it's dark out."

"It's safer when we're together, the three of us" Edmund tells me. "Safety in numbers, right?"

"Sure... Well, come on up."

Kalama exits the boat first, followed by her husband and then Edmund. Once Edmund steps aboard, the lights flicker a bit. They seem to go dim for a moment.

"Hope the wiring isn't going nutty," I say looking into the main light on the deck.

"Oh I'm sure it's probably nothing," Edmund smiles.

"Let's hope. Please, come in," I say holding the door to the living quarters open.

As the others take their seats I grab some mixed nuts to munch on. I offer coffee, but no one else seems interested.

"That was very kind of you to come to check on me so late."

"Oh, it's nothing," Edmund insists. "We just wanted to be sure you were okay since you didn't come back to camp."

"Yes, well, to be honest I thought I needed some time alone, but I am actually pretty thrilled to have you here now." I realize I mean that. It is nice to have the company.

"I hope we aren't intruding," Kalama chimes in.

"Not at all. I think having someone to talk to will do me good. I was feeling a little, well, off I guess, today — really lonely and insignificant, if that makes any sense."

"It saddens me to hear that. I know I haven't known you long, but for what it's worth I think you are an amazing individual," Edmund says.

"That's very kind," I blush.

"It's true. You must learn to accept yourself — your authentic self — faults and all. Embrace who you are and what you have, without needing to be more."

"I wish I could do that. I just feel like I fall short a lot, you know? In work, in my personal life, with my only living family even."

"You don't have to be perfect, you just have to give your best; that sound's like what you've been doing — you can't fault yourself for that. What you need, Lucas, is to let go of expectations, of who you think you should be. Embrace those qualities that make you the person you are."

"I don't know that I necessarily like those," I admit.

"Take the ones you do and nourish those. Be kind to yourself; show yourself some compassion."

"I try to do that. But I seem to fail miserably when it comes to making and keeping relationships."

"Hmm," Edmund cocks his head.

"You know, I'm starting to think there's something wrong with me. I mean, if you don't have deep, intimate, meaningful relationships, how can you be genuine?"

"That's right," Johnson finally contributes to the conversation.

"It's just hard for me. I lost my parents as a kid, you know... they both walked out. That made getting close to people terrifying. I lived life avoiding it so I wouldn't have to feel that kind of loss again. Now I feel that barrier I built is more crippling than loss could ever be."

"There's ways to shake loose that barrier, but first realize your past is just a story; that book was closed long ago — what remains of that story is what you must discern and transcend. You can open that book when you need to, pull out the lessons, then put it back on the shelf where it belongs. Reoccurring patterns are signs — notice them. Now, Mr. Psychology, you know how to treat avoidance behaviors, right?" Edmund stirs.

"Step into fear," Kalama bellows out like she's on some sort of game show. "I think that being a part of your community is important as well. I feel I belong here, on this island. Even if we are a very small community here, we are very connected. A few close friends is more soul enriching than a roomful of disengaged ones, I say."

"I agree completely," her husband says, as he moves in and rubs her shoulders gently. "We are all connected to everything else — other people, our planet, our community, our inner spirit, and to something greater than ourselves. Everything's connected. We are all *One*."

"That makes sense enough," I nod. "Our environment, its plants, and its animals energize us."

"They also make us compassionate and settle our minds," Edmund says.

"With relationships, all I know is that when things aren't working for us, it's usually because we have different goals or expectations, different values, or we're not spending enough time together," Kalama says. Johnson nods in agreement. The couple are sitting pressed-up next to each other and are holding hands. Their differences are no longer relevant, only harmony and love exists as they listen to what each other are saying.

"When we feel connected, we thrive," Johnson says, his eyes on his wife. They exchange a smile that is one I know they only use for one another. They look like a different couple than the one I met just the day before. The two turn their gaze to me and the smile is still there. They have included me in their moment — shared their love with me. The loneliness and triviality I felt out on the lagoon earlier vanishes.

As much as I enjoy the feeling of unity, it still makes me a bit squeamish. It isn't something I am too used to. Because of that, I say, "Are you all sure I can't get you something to drink? It doesn't have to be coffee — water, a glass of wine, some juice?"

"You've done plenty," Kalama grins. "Let me get them. I think I can find my way around, if you don't mind me digging around in the kitchen."

"Not at all. Glasses are above the sink."

Just as Kalama is opening the cabinet with the glasses, the boat goes dark.

"Oh, must be one of the breakers shorted out," I announce into the nearly pitch-black living quarters of the boat. "I'll just grab my flashlight and check."

The breaker isn't flipped, which is a little strange, but turning it off and then on again does the trick.

"Let there be light," I smile as the others blink at the florescent glow that fills the room again.

"That was easy enough," Edmund says.

"I'll get the drinks since I'm up," I tell Kalama. "What are we having, folks?"

"Actually, I think we'd probably better get going," Johnson says, standing and brushing the wrinkles out of his pants.

"Well that's too bad. Are you sure?"

"I would love to stay longer, but we promised Klara and Sawle we'd be back tonight."

"I'll let you go then, I guess," I joke. "Don't want them worrying about where you are too."

"It's been a nice visit," Edmund tells me as he boards his small boat. "I'm glad we came out to check on you."

"As am I," I concur. "I didn't realize it, but I needed it."

"We'll see you tomorrow then?" Kalama asks.

"Absolutely. Sleep well."

"And you do the same," Johnson says.

I reach to turn off the light in the sitting area and stop. I open the desk drawer to look at the picture one more time. It isn't there. I pull the drawer out as far as it will reach and shuffle the papers in it. Nothing. Someone took the photo. It must have happened while the lights were out. And to think, I was beginning to feel close to these people.

14

The thought of the missing picture nags at me and keeps me from falling asleep. Trying to turn my mind off now is an exercise in futility. Sitting on the sofa petting Blue, the scrolls in the picture flash in my mind. What in the world is on those scrolls? Something is obviously going on here that the others are hiding from me. I plan to figure out what, and now.

Since sleep is out of the question, I may as well solve this mystery. I'll go to the shack—Sawle's shack—while everyone else is asleep at the camp. I'll find out what everyone else seems to know that I don't. It's clear no one plans to tell me. If the others made it across the lagoon safely, I will too. I'll just take the panther the shaman gave me.

Out on the lagoon it is eerily quiet. The hum of the dinghy's motor bounces off the water and fills the thick air that hangs in the atmosphere. The metallic whine seems louder than usual against the silence of the night.

On shore I snap a leash on Blue. With the darkness and the spookiness of the island, I'm not taking any chances. I shine my flashlight ahead of us as we walk. Blue is nearly between my legs he's so close to me. The leash, it seems, is unnecessary.

"There it is," I whisper to Blue. Something about the whole thing makes me feel I need to be quiet—like I'm a kid sneaking out of the house at night while my parents doze in the next room.

Blue and I move slowly toward the shack. It looks more menacing in the dark of night. The Miracle Tree, the garden, everything that looked so peaceful and quaint now appears ominous in the shadows of nightfall. The harsh beams of the flashlight make everything look almost frightening as they settle on objects in the shack. A rustling of leaves and snapping of branches stops me. Blue growls a deep growl from his belly. My limbs turn to solid cement. My breath catches in my lungs and stays there. I force my hand with the flashlight to move. As the light escapes the door it travels out into a heavy mist that has descended on the island.

"It's nothing, guy. Only mist—that's all," I say to Blue as I scratch one of his ears, but I am really saying it for my own benefit.

I know that the heavy air outside the shack is nothing. As a man of science, I know that there is an explanation for it. It's just the humidity of the ocean coming to shore. Still, I am second-guessing my decision to go snooping around the atoll by myself in the middle of the night. I would give about anything to be safe on Betsy right now. I am losing my nerve.

Inhale. Big inhale. I take a deep breath, let it out, and wait for the cement to fall from my limbs. The breath caught in my lungs comes out. I continue my search. Beneath a crudely built desk is a scroll. I grab for it, almost reluctantly, and open it.

"This can't be real," I murmur, eyes fixed on the words before me. There, on the scroll, are intimate details about someone's life — my life. Details I have never told anyone on the island. I read things I have never told anyone, period. I read things about myself that not even I have come to terms with fully yet:

> *He is terrified of real relationships. He ended up being rejected, the one time he truly gave himself fully to someone after his parents abandoned him. His self-worth has been crushed. His failed marriage haunts him. His distant relationship with his sister and friends do too. Because of it, he believes that he is not worthy of love; that he is not worth knowing. He believes once people get to know him, they do not like him anymore — that he is faulty in some way. It is easiest for him to stay emotionally aloof than to step into his pain. Still he finds it isolating and lonely.*
>
> *He is in love with the one person he has in his life, a woman named Sam. He has never told her though. He believes earnestly Sam will disappear, one way or another, if he is ever honest. That she has never pursued him breaks his heart. He takes it as further proof that he is best to keep his distance.*
>
> *He struggles with some patients because they are brave enough to talk about the battles he fights himself. He envies their ability to cry over that which haunts them. He is conflicted — he wants to bury and expose his vulnerability simultaneously; and he is trying to do just that.*

"Who wrote this?" I say aloud. "Who wrote this about me? What is happening to me?"

ZZZZZ

The sunrise is beautiful. Even with so much going through my head, the pink-orange blaze lifting from the ocean calms me. The sound of footsteps behind me ruins the calm. It's Edmund.

"I need to talk to you," I say, brushing the sand from my backside as I get up. My clothes are damp. I don't care about that though.

"You're here early," he chirps merrily.

"I was here all night." The smile fades from Edmund's face.

"Is that right?"

"It is. And I found a scroll in the shack that..."

"You shouldn't have gone there. You weren't meant to see that yet," he interrupts. "I apologize that you did. It isn't the right time, Lucas."

"Who wrote it?"

"Listen, Lucas. I know this must be a bit strange."

"A bit strange?"

"Okay, yes... you're right. It's more than that. Just trust me. It will make sense when the time comes."

"Who wrote it?"

"Please, Lucas."

"Who?" I demand.

"Sawle did."

"Why? What are you people? What are you going to do to me?"

"Nothing bad. You've my word."

"Your word? I don't know what that's even worth."

"A lot, I think."

"Why is he writing about me?"

"You'll find out when you are ready."

"I'm ready now."

"You aren't," he insists.

"I am an adult, Edmund. I know what I am ready for. I want you to answer me right now."

"I'm sorry, Lucas. I just cannot do that. You just need to trust me."

"Right," I say, and take off for my boat.

"You aren't ready to leave yet," Edmund calls after me. I don't look back. Sam was right. Something is terribly wrong with this island. Something isn't right and I need to leave it as soon as I can.

Without knowing why, I stop. I take a breath and turn to ask, "Why did you take the photo?"

"The photo wasn't yours to take" he answers.

"Who are you? Who are all of you?"

"We're your friends, Lucas. I am telling you. This will make sense later."

"I want it to make sense right now."

"That is your problem, Lucas. You think that everything should make sense in life, but sometimes it just doesn't."

"You are hiding something from me and I want to know what," I bark.

"It is not the right time Lucas."

"Something isn't right and I'm supposed to let it be? That's bullshit. This is all bullshit: the weird nights here, the stuff laying around, the scrolls with stuff about me, the photos that make no sense. This entire island is bullshit!"

"Please, listen to me, Lucas..."

"I'm trying to! But you won't tell me anything!"

"I will tell you this Lucas. Not everything in life is perfect. Not everything in life makes sense. But realize that everything is as it should be. You must learn to surrender to what is and let it be until it's time."

"Cop out."

"You're so skeptical of everyone. If you don't get it the first time, you are done. That is your problem. You need to. . ."

"To what?" I demand.

"You need to mind your own business and surrender to what is."

"This is my business. Those scrolls were about *me!*"

"And you will know when it is time why those scrolls are there," Edmund says very firmly. He's as intense as I've ever seen him. "But right now understand this; there is beauty in not knowing. With or without the knowledge you want right now, things are beautiful. Look around you."

"I need some time," I say, getting my boat into the lagoon with my back to Edmund.

"Of course," he says, his voice becoming soft again. "This is a lot."

"Maybe this trip was a mistake," I grumble as I start the engine to the small boat.

"There aren't mistakes; except when you push life. Then it will push back," he says stoically.

"We'll see."

"You will. I promise," Edmund says, and then turns and walks away.

Watching Edmund disappear into the jungle of the island, I decide not to go back to Betsy just yet. I putt back to shore and Blue and I hop out onto the beach. Blue grabs a nearby piece of driftwood and sets it down at my feet—his way of trying to lighten the mood.

"Why not," I smile at him. After a few throws Blue loses interest and so do I. I sit down on the white sand and look out into the ocean. Sitting quietly, I feel the love of the sun and gentle embrace of the sea breeze. I feel a little guilty for being so harsh with Edmund. I just don't understand why, or what even, he is keeping from me. I don't like feeling that I'm the only one who doesn't know something. I cannot get the thought of that manuscript out of my mind. Seeing those words that were written about me stirs up a little heat in my chest again. What are these people working at here?

"Maybe what Edmund is saying is right," I say to Blue, who has collapsed beside me in the sand. "Maybe I should trust him and let things unfold as they should." Blue raises his head and licks my arm.

I know I must learn to surrender my insecurities or I'll be struggling with them like I always have. The problem is, I haven't quite figured out how to do that. I'm also torn about how I feel about this atoll and its inhabitants altogether. One minute I feel as close as family, and the next I realize I hardly know these people at all.

An unsettling feeling suddenly hits me. I know this feeling. It is the feeling you get when someone is watching you. I can almost feel the gaze searing through me. Scanning the horizon for the set of eyes that is triggering my unease, I notice that Blue has stopped gnawing on a stick and has zeroed in on something. His eyes look right past me. He sees something behind me. I see his upper lip curl and hear a growl. My blood goes chilly and my face feels numb. Blue is now on his feet, hair bristled and ears pinned down to his skull. I slowly turn to face whatever it is he sees.

It's no one. I look back at Blue and then to the place he has his eyes set on. Still nothing is there. Leaving Blue, I follow his gaze almost into the tree line, but it is obvious no one is here. Blue must have seen a bird or some small animal. I am relieved that there is no one here, but can't shake an underlying sense of agitation. I almost would rather see someone standing there. That would at least explain Blue's behavior and my gut feeling that someone was spying on me.

"It's nothing, buddy," I say to Blue. I notice as I lean down to pet him a piece of opal-like crystal sitting right where I was just moments before. Examining the small stone, I realize it is just like the deposits I saw in the cave my first day on the atoll. It is the mineral that Edmund told me they use to purify the water they drink. It's the only piece here, and the cave is nowhere nearby. I know that it wasn't here when I sat down. Someone put it there. They had to have.

"I know you're trying to tell me something!" I yell out into the universe as I pivot around to see if anyone is there. "What are you trying to show me? Just show me, dammit!" I cry out.

Silence. There is nothing but silence in return. I drop to the sand and something takes hold of me. I hear a noise again and realize it is me. It's my voice. I am sobbing. I open my eyes and the sand is damp where my tears have fallen. I cannot remember the last time I truly cried. Strangely I feel, alive. My muscles contract and relax and I can feel my pulse everywhere in my body. My sobs release something that has been building all day — maybe all week, or a lifetime for all I know.

I snap back to the moment, raise myself up from the sand, and wipe my eyes. My eyes, still a little blurry and hot from crying, drift to one side. Through the fog of residual tears I see footprints on the shore. They aren't mine, I know. Were they there before and I missed them?

I inhale deeply, get my composure back, and take off following the footprints. Blue stays right beside me as I walk. The prints go off into the lush, thick green of the atoll. I continue, my eyes on the ground. The tracks take me to the thick groves and Pisonias.

Squinting to see the tracks in the shade of the groves, my ears prick at the sound of rustling grass behind me. That feeling I had on the beach that someone was watching me is back. It consumes me. Now that I'm in the belly of the island, it terrifies me. Someone is spying on me. I suddenly get the sense that I have fallen into their trap. I feel my pupils swell and a cold sweat cover my entire body. I have to find someone to help me.

"Come on, Blue," I blurt, and take off to the interior of the jungle. "Hurry, Blue. Please, hurry!" I pant.

My feet pound against the earth beneath me. The echoes of my frenzied steps fill my brain. *Go!* I tell myself. *Go!* I try to keep my eyes forward, but I see a shadow drifting between the trees just beside me. *Come on, Lucas! You have to get to camp!*

I do not want to turn to see what is moving along beside me. My heart is in a marathon and my nerves are about to shake everything inside me out. *Eyes forward. Just keep your eyes forward*, and then my head snaps to the side to look. The shadow is gone. I keep at a dead sprint. My eyes shoot forward, and then back to the trees. Nothing.

All of a sudden my foot throbs. My ankle buckles and my body slams to the ground. The wind is knocked out of me. Someone grabbed my foot!

Scrambling to my feet, I pant, "no, no, no." My eyes dart in every direction. Who just grabbed me? Picking my foot up I realize it was no one. A vine caught my boot and tripped me. I break free of the vine and work back into a dead run. It may have not been a person that grabbed my foot, but I still have the overwhelming sense that someone is there, not far from me; someone who doesn't want me there.

A few hundred feet into the jungle, I finally stop running when I see a familiar face. It is Dr. Judd. He's at what appears to be a well, gathering water. The serene look on his face seems completely out of place for the way I feel. He is whistling, dropping a bucket slowly into a well. I notice the well is made of the same crystal that was in the cave. It is the same crystal that I found back on shore. The well also has the word, or maybe the initials, *AJA* etched into the side.

"Dr. Judd, there's something out there..." I wheeze once I am in earshot of the doctor.

"You're alright, Lucas," Judd replies calmly.

"No, there's something out there. It was like I... I went after it, but then it started chasing me. It was like... Wait, were you out on the beach earlier?"

"I'm sure I was," he says without looking up from the well.

"Were you there when I was there?"

"I could have been. I don't know when you were there."

"I mean did you happen to see me out there today, because I swear someone was watching me. And then I was running and this shadow..."

"Here, take this," Judd interrupts handing me a black crystal he just pulled from his pocket.

"And do what with it?"

"Place that black crystal on the ground. Tell me, what do you see?"

At that moment, the rays of the sun illuminate the white sand through a gap in the leaves of the jungle foliage. The light encases the black crystal. It seems but a speck amidst the glowing light of the sand.

"That's amazing," I mumble, a little awestruck. "There will always be light and darkness in life..."

"And the darkness will always be there—but is not always powerful. The only strength it gets is what we give it," Dr. Judd finishes my thought. "When we choose to live a heart-centered life, we have chosen to live in the light," he adds.

"I suppose we do," I agree, my eyes still fixed on the crystal and the sand.

"Our emotional pain, our doubts and fears, all these things stand in the way of where we are and the deeper selves we want to be."

"Sure," I concur.

"Inner peace is the state in which we learn to embrace the negative as much as we do the positive, accepting them as part of us. It is only natural to avoid less pleasant emotions, but the solution is not to look for ways to throw off those feelings but to achieve harmony with them. Do you hear what I'm saying, Lucas?"

"I think I do. What you're saying is that inner peace is a state of complete harmony, where our internal self is balanced both in mind and spirit," I reply as I lean back against the well.

"That's right," Judd smiles, looking satisfied with my observation.

"But how do I heal and get to that place of inner peace?" I ask.

"There's no one way or right way. You choose your way—through prayer, meditation, or yoga, or maybe even escaping to a secluded island," he answers as he looks my way with smiling eyes. "Whatever your way is, inner peace is found by allowing yourself time to quietly self-reflect on your inner dialogue and the emotions you carry about the experiences in your life. By practicing mindfulness, we can better understand the teachings of the heart, and better manage the unconstructive thoughts that hinder our growth and expansion."

"Hmmm."

"By observing, assimilating and balancing our thoughts, we heighten our conscious awareness and begin living a higher way," he explains.

"I'd like to know then, can we grow without experiencing pain? I've had enough hurt and suffering."

"Absolutely," the doctor tells me. "Listen, as a physician and a missionary, I've seen plenty of people in pain. What I began to notice is that much of it comes from stress—much of it self-inflicted."

"As a psychologist, I can agree with that."

"But when it does come from external forces, like the plague or cholera for example, it boils down to our ability to keep both our immunity and mind strong, which can overcome many dis-eases."

"You believe that then?"

"With my whole being I do," he replies, his eyes intense and countenance serious. "When it comes to matters of the heart, we can grow through the experiences of both love and pain. But there is a shift. A shift away from the historic pain-centered growth of power and conquest, to that of growing through love, awareness, and understanding —humanity is evolving much like everything else."

"I would love to believe that, but do you think that is a reality?"

"Society is evolving, Lucas. Look how much things have flourished just these past 100 years. It is when we stop listening to our soul and stop trusting our higher guidance, that we believe we need pain and struggle to grow. It's when we follow our joy that the true essence of our life unfolds. When we focus on that which feels good and serves the greater good, we resonate with love and grow in a more enlightened way," Judd explains, and then his expression lightens and a smile creeps onto his face. "Now how about that fishing trip I promised you?" he asks jovially.

"Fishing?"

"Why not?"

"We were kind of in a deep talk here," I say, confused by his sudden change of focus.

"And we can't talk while we fish?" he asks.

"Not a bad idea I guess. But really quickly..."

"Yes?"

"What does A-J-A stand for?"

"Excuse me?"

"On the well there," I say, pointing at the inscription on the well, "it says A-J-A. Any idea what that comes from?"

"Ah, that. It is *Aja*, a word, not an acronym. It means spirit of the forest, the animals within it, and herbal healers. It's Yoruba I believe."

"I wonder why it is on the well?"

"Who knows?" Judd shrugs. "Maybe it will click later. That happens sometimes."

"Hmm."

"So fishing then?"

"Yes, fishing," I say.

"I can grab the gear if you just want to wait here," Judd says.

"You sure? I can help."

"No need. I know where everything is. It'll just be a bit."

"I'll be here then."

It hits me as Judd disappears into a hut that I am all alone. Blue is not by my side as usual. I look around, but he is nowhere.

"Blue!" I call out and listen for his panting or the rustling of the grass. Dead silence is all I hear. "Blue!" I yell louder as anxiety wells up in my guts. Still, nothing. Blue is gone.

"Everything okay?" Judd asks as he emerges with poles and a tackle box in hand.

"It's Blue," I gasp. "It's. . . he is gone. He always comes to his name. He's. . ."

"When did you see him last?"

"I guess back when I was running, before I came up on you. He must've disappeared when I was running from the shadows. We have to find him, Dr. Judd!"

"Let's just calm down."

"I'm not going anywhere until I find Blue. We have to find him," I insist.

"We'll find him. Let's not get too riled. We'll just retrace your steps," Judd suggests calmly.

I take off in the direction of the well, shouting for Blue incessantly as I walk. Every ten feet or so I stop to listen for him. I go back to the area I tripped and fell.

"Blue, boy!" I shout desperately. "Come on, buddy!" I plead. "Please, Blue, please be okay," I whimper and drop to the ground.

My body is weighed down by fear and hopelessness just thinking about all the things that could have happened to Blue. I feel water in my eyes picturing him hurt and alone somewhere. Then I take a deep breath and close my eyes. I slow my thoughts down. Nothing has happened yet. Blue could just as well be caught up chasing an island rodent, blissfully unaware of my calls. I am only focusing on the negative stuff. That is my problem.

I take a chance and *surrender* to the spirit within me and to whatever else is out there — I let it take my worry and angst. A few minutes pass as I kneel on the moist ground beneath me; then a sense of calm wraps itself around me. I can see Blue, smell him, almost touch his soft ears with my mind. I open my eyes. Blue will be fine — I know it. He is always fine. I pick myself up and set out to find Dr. Judd.

"I think we should go back to Sky and wait there," I say when I spot Judd out searching for Blue in the thick trees of the island.

"Are you sure?"

"I am. He'll come back. He knows where camp is."

"If he doesn't show up by this afternoon, we'll come out again," Judd says.

"Okay."

A heaviness settles on me again as I walk. I want to believe Blue is fine. I want to believe that by tomorrow all this will seem trivial — the worry and the panic. But a foreboding sense of loss is roused inside me the closer we get to camp. It's that nagging feeling I've had my whole life. It's the feeling that was ingrained on my psyche the day I stood at my grandpa's graveside and watched him disappear into the earth; and maybe even before that — I never got over mom walking out and dad giving up.

I don't say much as we walk. Neither does Dr. Judd. I vacillate between hope and fear. It seems that every step I take brings me to a new emotion. Calm washes over me, and then panic bubbles up. I smile thinking of Blue standing at the bottom of a giant Pisonia, barking his head off at a bird that sits and teases him. The next second I see him hurt and wondering where I am and my heart sinks. I'm pulled away from my fickle daydreams when we come to a steep, rocky path.

"Do you notice how this path is a bit like life Lucas?" Dr. Judd inquires as we work our way up the unsteady course. "With each step we take, we get closer to where we need to be."

"But when we can't see the end, we sometimes get nervous about what is on the other side," I add, thinking about Blue and my fears.

"Just keep your eyes open and feet moving forward," he smiles, putting a hand on my shoulder.

I look at Judd and return his smile, then look forward to see that we are to a point where we can now see further into the distance. My eyes fall on a tremendous obstacle. There before me is a river — a river much too wide and moving much too fast for us to swim.

"I thought you knew where we're going," I say looking out on the body of water in front of us.

"Sure I do, but you won't always have someone showing you the way, Lucas."

"But you're here right now, aren't you?"

"Trust your inner guide to show you the way; no matter the obstacle. So, which way, Captain?" he says with his hands stretched out in front of him. My eyes are drawn to a rocky cliff that seems to be climbable, not too far beyond some low-hanging trees that look to be as old as the ones near the field of butterflies.

"Good choice... Come this way," he gestures to follow him off the path.

Judd takes me to a tunnel I hadn't noticed from where we were on the path. It is in the rock face. When we go into it, I feel the same way I did when I visited the Louvre once. It is beautiful. On the other side of the tunnel we come to an area with beautiful green plants and vibrant flowers in a range of colors that pop and glow in the sunlight. There is a small waterfall not too far in front of us that drops into a beautiful lake at the bottom. The waters of the fall create ripples that ease out into the smooth, calm lake. It is a mirror for the skies above. The place exudes peace and tranquility.

"You see this?"

"Of course I do."

"Do you know what it means?"

"Not really," I admit, still in awe of my surroundings.

"Sometimes there's great beauty waiting on the other side of an obstacle, Lucas."

"I will say it. I did not expect this, at all."

"We hardly ever do. Our minds get too caught in the trial. We forget the big picture. Sometimes this is what an interrupted path leads us to."

"This place is something right out of a dream," I gawk.

"Kind of. When you've drunk it all in, we best get back to camp."

"Oh, yes, right. Let's get going, then. We've still got fishing to do while we wait for Blue."

The smell of campfire fills my nostrils as we come up on the camp. Coming into the main area I see a line of fish cleaned and ready to fry. It appears someone else got to the fishing before we did. I am a little relieved. Truth be told, I want to stay in one place so Blue can find me.

"Looks like someone did the fishing already," I nod toward the fish that glistens in the high noon sun.

"It would appear so," Judd chuckles. "Less work for us I guess. No need for us to go if it's done."

I nod in agreement. Judd goes into his hut to put his gear away.

I notice Captain Sawle near the fire pit grilling some of the fish. "Eat up, no need to wait for me," Judd says.

I sit by myself at a table. I stare out into the jungle of the atoll, squinting to see if I might see Blue pouncing through.

15

"What are you doing here by yourself?" a familiar voice asks. It's Klara; she is walking towards me. She looks more ethereal than ever as she glides across the ground in her loose-fitting white frock, her silver hair reflecting the soft island sunlight. "And where's Blue?"

"He's gone. He disappeared in the jungle. I need to find him," I tell her as my eyes dart around the groves of thick trees that stand tall and daunting all around us. Just saying out loud that Blue is missing stirs up the anxiety that still lingers in me.

"You have fear in your heart, Lucas. You feared losing Blue from the moment you arrived on the island."

"How do you know that? I never said that."

"I don't need your words to tell me that," she says, her eyes fixed on me as I squirm a bit under her iron gaze. "What happened when Blue disappeared? What did you feel?" she asks.

"I was running from a shadow. I was afraid."

"When we believe what fear tells us, we manifest that reality."

"I suppose that makes sense," I agree, pondering that notion a moment.

"Remember our talk on the boat, Lucas?"

"Sure."

"I told you then that the sharks won't hurt you when your heart and intentions are pure. It's a part of the harmony that exists. Just as the island has restored balance, so must you. Do you hear what I'm saying to you?"

"I think so," I say, but I don't know that I do completely.

"Walk in the light and the dark can never hurt you," Klara says to me.

We stand silent, neither of us breaking our stare. As I look into her soft, blue eyes I can see her passion. Her eyes, which are the most intense I have seen them, swim in their sockets. The tears that glaze her eyes make them seem brighter than any blue I've seen; bluer than the Pacific that surrounds us; bluer than the sky that resides overhead. Before she can reach out to scoop me into her grandmotherly grip, I reach out my arms to her. She collapses into my embrace. Her warmth and energy are loving. I can feel it permeate my own existence as we stand there, intertwined. And then she steps back and without a word turns to go to her cabin.

"Thank you, Klara," I say in a voice so low it is almost a whisper.

She turns around with shining eyes to tell me, "Blue is fine." Her reassurance comforts me. She has already turned around again, but I wave to her anyway and smile.

Once Klara disappears into her cabin, I make my way over to the fire, which Captain Sawle stands stoically over like a Queen's Guard over Buckingham Palace. He stokes the fire, and I try to see what he's got cooking. As I plant myself beside the captain and steal a look over his shoulder,

Edmund walks over from the path between the cabins. I notice his clothes are damp and then my eyes drop to his shoes, which are covered in sand; probably the dirt as he walked in his wet, hemp shoes.

"I just went for a swim but didn't have a towel to dry off with," Edmund announces, likely because he's noticed my curious stare.

"Hmm," I grunt in return.

"I heard Blue has gone missing. Klara just told me," he says. "Let's eat up and I'll help you find him."

"Thanks, man," I say.

Edmund, Sawle, and I all sit down to eat. We sit on a small grassy area at the edge of the lodge for a change, to get some sun. The others must be busy because they don't join us. That is fine because we are all gobbling our food down as quickly as possible. Even though I'm hardly taking the time to chew my food, I notice how tasty it is.

"It's very good," I say with my mouth full of fish.

"The spices are from my garden," he replies. "So are the berries and greens in the salad."

"You've done a great job," I mumble over my mouthful of food. "It must taste even better to you since you grew it."

"It does," he says.

We finish up and Edmund and I walk towards the camp I set up near Betsy; the Captain catches up. I notice paw prints on the ground. The tracks circle one another in different directions and look erratic. I feel my food sitting right at the back of my throat suddenly.

"He was scared," I announce with my eyes cast downward toward the prints. "I can tell Blue was scared and trying to find his way home."

"We'll find him," Captain Sawle says.

The three of us take to following the prints like a pack of bloodhounds with serious sinus infections, using our eyes instead of our sense of smell to find our missing person. I belt out Blue's name over and over as we walk, three abreast, along the beach. All of a sudden the paw prints disappear and we lose the trail.

"He must've gone back into the thick," I sigh.

"We can go back to the campsite on the beach. If he was there before, he may be there now waiting," Edmund suggests. Sawle and I nod simultaneously in agreement and follow him back.

"He still isn't here," I groan desperately as I stare at the empty camp near Strawn Island, not far from Betsy. I want to scream, at Edmund, at Sawle, at God, and even at Blue for disappearing. I feel my teeth clench, my jaw is set hard in place. My head is a pressure cooker. But then I see something.

There's a man-made pier nearby. It's made of local wood and looks far older than anyone on the island. It was probably built during World War II by some sailors. Though it is splintered and weather-beaten, it still looks sturdy enough to walk on. It looks like the kind of place Blue and I could have a lot of fun on, if only he'd find his way back to us.

I take several deep breathes and head for the pier. The anxiety subsides as I walk and breathe in deeply. I feel that the others are following my lead. When we are all standing at the edge of the old battered platform, we plop down, almost in chorus, on the edge.

"You swim in your clothes often?" I ask Edmund, grinning as I look him up and down. His clothes are still not dry. "You didn't expect me to believe your no towel story earlier did you?"

"Sure I did... you *are* on a tropical island, remember," Edmund retorts. "There are very few rules here. Being here isn't like being back home. You can do as you please and when you please—even swim in your clothes if the mood hits you."

Edmund lets out a chuckle as he nudges me into the water. I don't try too hard to keep myself from plunging into the lagoon beneath us. *Splash!* I hit the water and let myself sink a bit before I bob back up to the surface. When I emerge from beneath, I see Edmund laughing from the pier.

"Might as well join me," I call out, and Edmund jumps in, shoes and all. Captain Sawle stays planted on the dock, a friendly but serious gargoyle keeping watch.

Thrashing around in the lagoon seems to lighten the mood. It feels great to swim and splash around in the crystal clear waters. I see no sharks. I feel *alive*. Strangely, this is the first time for me to swim since arriving on Palmyra. The smell of saltwater and the coolness of the lagoon on my skin make me suddenly nostalgic. I remember what its like to be a child again and have fun. It has been ages since I thought about the good memories of my childhood. I've spent my life letting tragedy eclipse the excitement and joy I felt when I was young. One memory in particular sweeps over me.

My Grandma Gladys used to take my sister Leah and I to the Rock Pool at Malibu Creek. The two of us always had a blast there as kids, messing around in the water and climbing over the ancient volcanic rock. We played King of the Mountain. Sometimes Leah became a mermaid and

I a cantankerous pirate, out for treasure or revenge. Mostly, we laughed. We felt close to one another and nothing but the joy of the moment existed. Right now, I feel just like that.

"You seem more relaxed now," Edmund announces over the splashing of the water, interrupting my nostalgic thoughts.

"I am," I reply thoughtfully with a grin.

I plunge down below the surface for an underwater swim. I kick my legs and vent my arms through the cool water. I head for the sands of the beach and stay under water until the lagoon bottom lifts to meet me. Popping up from my swim I hear a sound that stops me from taking a breath. It's the sound of an excited dog panting and pouncing on damp sand. Blue is standing in the surf right in front of me, wagging his tail ferociously as he bounces to and fro like a wind up toy that never quits, calling out to me in an excited whine.

"Blue, buddy!" I shout as a run for him. "Blue, you amazing, frustrating, dog! Oh, Blue! I could kill you if I didn't want to hug you so much!"

Suddenly we take on the look of long lost friends reunited after a war, running at each other on the beach of a beautiful Pacific island. Blue meets me halfway and I collapse on top of him, wrapping my arms around his body, which quivers and shakes in my grasp from all the excitement. I pull him into my chest and give him a bear hug and then pull away so I can give him a good scratch from head to toe. My heart is heavy with gratitude that I've got my best friend back, and he even seems to be unscathed.

The things that matter the most are the one's we love.

As Blue buries his head into my wet clothes, his wagger still going strong, a strange feeling comes over me. I close my eyes for a moment and I see that cave again—the one I took the fall in when I first landed on the island. The cave I found when I first went looking for Blue. My body is right there with Blue on the beach, but my consciousness, my mind, is back in the cave again. The air around me gets thin and the light more intense. Everything feels like an echo. My muscles begin to burn with weakness and my head feels strange. It's as though my soul is lifting from me, going back to the cave and leaving my body there on the beach with Blue.

"Are you alright Lucas?" Edmund asks as he walks up to me from the lagoon.

"It's the cave... where I met you... there's something there. There's something wrong," I tell Edmund. My skin feels numb now. It's like that dead finger trick kids used to do in grade school. I know that I am still petting Blue, but the sensation of his fur on my fingers and palms has vanished.

"You'll be alright Lucas, just relax and breathe," Edmund instructs.

"Right," I mumble. I lean back on my haunches and suck in the fresh, saline air. In, out; I fill my lungs, hold the breath, and blow it from me as if it were a drag off a Cuban cigar. A few deep breathes later, my senses start to return. I can feel Blue's coarse hair and my head clears.

"There's something I need to show you, Lucas" Edmund says as he waves a hand motioning for me to come with him.

"Let's go, Bud," I say to Blue as I chase after Edmund.

He leads me through the dense foliage back to that majestic waterfall that Dr. Judd showed me earlier. I didn't even realize that we were in the same place until the cascading water was gushing before my eyes yet again.

"Look around you," Edmund says without looking at me. "What do you see?"

"Nature," I respond, with the inflection of a question rather than the certainty of a statement.

"What does it *mean* though?" Edmund pushes.

"Nature?"

"Yes. What does it all mean?"

"I guess life," I answer, feeling like I've been hit with a pop quiz.

"You're on the right track," Edmund smiles. "The trees there in the ground, those are symbols. And so is the water, both the fall and the pool it collects in. Look at them, Lucas, and wait for the significance to hit you."

My eyes settle on the towering Pisonias. I drop my head back to follow the great structures to their peek that sways so many feet above us. Their age has given them wisdom and patience, with themselves and with life around them. They stand tall and watch over the island, keeping it cool and providing both shelter and food for the life here. When it was young, it protected itself and scolded the animals that nibbled its leaves and used its branches. Now that it has had time, it lends itself to all that need it. It has become a part of the vitality of the island. The tree works best when it is offering itself to better the lives of others.

Those letters, AYA, that I saw on the well the day before flash in my mind. My thoughts are no longer mine.

There is something more powerful at work—a knowing that has settled on me. The concept of AYA becomes apparent to me. *It is the spirit of the forest, the animals within it, and herbal healers*—I am here for them, as much as they are here for me. It is everything working with one another to flourish; a circular cohabitation which thrives when everything works together for the good of the whole. My existence is one with the whole.

"We begin living our higher purpose when we live with love and gratitude in our heart. There is a spirit in everything—within us, all around us," Edmund tells me.

I remain silent. I look to the waterfall now as the fall gushes and gurgles as it meets the small lake at its base. The fall feeds the lake, which quenches the thirst of the animals. Water is the most vital element to life. This water keeps life going—the wildlife, the aquatic life, and the vegetation all around me. The lake wouldn't exist if the stream above it didn't pump fresh water into it constantly. Without the stream and the fall, the lake would become stagnant—a breeding ground for sickness and disease instead of life and vitality. It is the movement that keeps it going. It needs constant movement, just as we need constant movement by growth. If we stand still, we become stagnant. We cannot nurture anything, especially ourselves, if we cannot move forward.

The thinness of the air comes again. My thoughts are muddled with a fog, but the fog lifts. My head clears, but I can sense a shift. Something isn't right again, but I don't feel that it is Palmyra anymore. That uneasy feeling that has plagued me isn't the result of this island. It's me. My head pounds and my eyes lose focus. All around me I see nothing but ambiguous streaks of green, blue, and brown.

What's going on?

The numbness that plagued my hands earlier spreads through my body. I am as weightless and light as a helium balloon. Things are coming into and dropping out of focus around me. Blue is here and then gone. Edmund's voice is wafted away in a breeze. I hear him call, but he's at the end of a long tunnel and the words never find their way to me. I can no longer tell what is real and what isn't. I am drowning in my own consciousness.

16

In the obscurity of the moment, I hear Captain Sawle's voice. It booms against my eardrums, but it is also muddled. The captain calls out from nearby to Edmund.

"It's time to go, Edmund," he says.

I muster up all the strength I have and force a strained, an almost desperate, "Where are you going?"

"It's time for us to go now, Lucas. You're going to be okay, do not worry. But we must leave now."

"Leave what?"

"Leave you."

"Why are you leaving me here? I don't. . ."

"I know," Edmund cuts me off. "We can't stay. . . Everything will be alright."

Edmund and Captain Sawle disappear within the deep greens of the atoll. As they get further away, I gather myself and stand up. My head is still swimming, but it is at least in shallower waters.

"Blue," I blurt, panicked, but Blue's cold nose on my hand soothes my nerves.

I blink a few times to get my vision back into focus. I can still see the two figures, but barely. *Where are they going? And why have they left me alone? I need to know. I have to follow them.*

"We've got to be quiet, Blue," I say, leaning over to look at Blue in the eyes. He responds to my order by leaning in and letting his rough tongue glide across my cheek. We head off to track the two.

I need to hang back so Edmund and Sawle won't catch on. I keep my distance. In the thick of the foliage, though, it gets harder and harder to keep an eye on the men; they're too far away. Not ten minutes in, the images disappear completely. They are now lost in the thick jungle viscera.

"We'll just wait for them back at Sky then," I say to Blue.

In no time we're back at the lodge, and Blue is clinging to me like a newborn pup to his mother. I nearly trip over him as I pace the compound, looking for signs of anyone.

"Klara?" I call into her cabin. "Are you in there?" Only silence answers me.

"Klara?" I call again, "I could really use an ear right now. Edmund and Sawle are acting..."

The door to Klara's cabin is ajar, so I lightly nudge it open with the toe of my hiking boot. The door whines and squeals as it slowly swings open. When it finally comes to rest, my heart stops. Klara's cabin is empty —completely empty. There is no sign that anyone has been in it for ages.

I step into the cabin and do a clumsy pirouette to scan the entire place. There isn't a stick of furniture in it. Has she not been sleeping in her own cabin this whole time?

With an intense uneasiness growing inside me, I burst out of Klara's cabin and head for Edmund's. I stand at his door and call in.

"Edmund, are you back?" I call. Again, silence.

Edmund's door is closed, so I grab the door handle and twist it hard to open it. The handle sticks. I have to put my shoulder into the door to get it to open. I can only nudge it slightly, but enough to squeeze inside. His cabin is deserted also! Consternation consumes me on the spot.

They're all gone! It's like they were never even there. It makes no sense at all. How did they all pack up so quickly? And why? What is going on here? I'm starting to think that Klara's hug was really a goodbye.

A dreadful chill colder than death itself works its way from the balls of my feet to the crown of my head, tickling my spine as it travels. Panic hits me so hard it nearly paralyzes me. There is something not right here; something terribly amiss—Sam was right. I have got to get back to Betsy!

"Come on, Blue," I gasp as I stumble backwards out of Edmund's cabin, which is as desolate as a forgotten countryside cemetery, and just as unnerving.

I run. I run fast, through the heavy shrubs and plant life that seem to be grabbing at my boots and pulling at my legs. A surge of panic burns through me as I feel dampness cover my body. I recite the words, "come on Blue" over and over like a Gregorian chant as I slash through the jungle. I time the words with the pounding of my feet, which happens to match the hard knocking on my ribcage. I am nearly out of the suffocating flora when I see the sun sinking below the horizon.

"No!" I gasp.

I break through the last section of lush green and collapse on the sand. I want to move—to keep going until I get to the boat—but my muscles are worn to their limits. My legs throb with exhaustion. I get to my feet and take a step. I might as well be walking against the current of the Amazon after monsoon season.

"No," I whisper as I drop my head to the sand. "The fog. Help!" I call out, knowing no one is going to come to my aid now.

As helpless as an infant, I roll over on my back, panting, and look back at the island. There is no fog there, though —no shadows or sinister forces hovering above me. The island is quiet behind me, even peaceful. There is no one here but me and Blue—nothing good or bad, just us. My muscles go soft and my mind clears. I fall back on the sand and let out a half-sigh, half-chuckle. Calm sets in and swallows me up. I let it. I close my eyes and drift away on a current of tranquility.

ZZZZZ

I open my eyes and I am in the cave again. I can feel the cool earth beneath me; I smell the dirt and feel the grittiness of it under my body. I feel Blue by my side. His warm tongue bathes my cheek again. He whines at me, and I close my eyes. Again, I feel that I am adrift in some unknown body of water.

As I come to, I can sense that someone other than Blue is nearby; it's the shaman. He is hovering over me. I can feel his stare on me. It's as heavy as an anvil.

"Oh, am I happy to see you," I say, relieved to see a familiar face and someone that can explain what is happening.

"Be calm. You no longer need to fear, Lucas," the shaman says. "The energy you had manifested, that of fear, of loss, of abandonment—that is what drew the darkness to you. You can now let it go—all that you need is now within you. You have your teachings. Now go forward with courage."

"What do you mean? That *I* caused those things? All of them?"

"Yes," he nodded.

"I couldn't have," I argued.

"Blue getting lost and the poison fish, those were your own doubts and mistrust coming to pass. The marriage that ended was the manifestation of your fear of loss. That same fear is the reason you are so isolated and have few friends."

"I..."

"Just wait," the shaman stops me. "Let me finish. And let yourself take in what I say before you respond. People too often listen, only so they can reply; instead of listening to understand. Now hear what I am saying..."

"Okay."

"Okay," he nodded and continued. "Your mind—what you choose to believe and listen to—and your soul have always guided your human experience. When you stop believing in the Light and stop living from the heart, that's when darkness walks in. Your soul has been clouded by your emotional pain and negative beliefs; which is why you've failed to trust it. You must return to living with your heart. All that you do and do not have right now, is your creation. What future will you create from this point forward, Lucas?"

"While you think, know this... you don't need the answers to those three questions you came here seeking. *Just never stop seeking! That's where your answers are hidden. Trust in the Great Spirit. Your deeper purpose and meaning will unfold in their own time,*" he adds.

I nod, lie back, and drift off again until I hear another voice calling my name. It isn't the shaman, though, or Klara, or Edmund, or anyone else on the island. The voice is feminine. It sounds so familiar. The voice sounds like

Sam's. But that can't be. I'm hallucinating. I'm dreaming that Sam is here.

"Hello?" I call back, even though I know I can't be hearing Sam.

"Lucas?" the voice calls again. "Lucas, it's Sam. Where are you?"

"The cave," I shout, but my voice is weak. Blue begins to bark. He knows Sam's voice well.

I hear footsteps approaching then metallic clanging bouncing off the cave walls. Blue darts away from me and returns with Sam. That can't be though. There is no way Sam could be there. I just talked to her.

"Oh my God, Lucas," Sam sobs as she falls down beside me. "Lucas, Lucas, Lucas."

She scoops my head in her hands and cradles me like I'm an infant, smoothing my hair back from my face. Her tears begin to soak my face. I realize though they are mixed with my own. I am crying with her, but I don't I know why.

"What are you doing here?" I finally ask. "What is going on?"

"We came to find you," she says as she helps me sit up. "I can't believe we did."

"Who did?"

"The search party," she says, and I see a group of three men and two women in a cluster behind her. They all look as though they were expecting to rescue me from the side of a mountain, with ropes, quickdraws, and carabiners dangling from them like rustic ornaments from an adventure themed Christmas tree.

"I don't understand," I mutter, suddenly realizing how stiff I am. "I just talked to you. I told you..."

I lay my head down again and close my eyes, waiting to wake from the dream. I must be hallucinating and I need to find the others. Something is terribly wrong. Did I eat something poisonous again? If so, I need to find the shaman and quick. I need someone who is really there to come to my aid. Hallucinations of my best friend are not going to save my life, and I know that.

17

I open my eyes and I'm in a strange place. I'm aboard a boat, but it isn't Betsy; its someone else's boat. I gaze around the cabin, blinking hard into the artificial light that buzzes around me. Sam is next to me holding my hand. She's still here. Am I still dreaming?

"Lucas, you're alright now. We found you," Sam says. "Thank God, we found you!"

I can feel Sam's hand on mine. I also feel a throbbing in my head. Everything seems too real to be a dream. I can smell the familiar smell of Sam's shampoo — she's used mango papaya shampoo since we were in college — as she leans close to me. I grope at my own body to make sure that I am here; and that this is all really happening. My head feels like its full of wet pillow stuffing and sand and my body aches — all over.

"What happened to me?" I finally ask and notice a thick film on my extremely chapped lips.

"I'm not sure. We found you lying on the ground, disoriented and dazed near a cave."

"Those people with the dangling climbing gear; they were real then?"

"Yes," Sam smiles sweetly. "They are out checking Betsy now to make sure she's locked up."

"I don't think I am all here yet," I admit. "I am still not quite sure how you got here, or how I got here for that fact."

"You were drifting in and out of consciousness. It took us a couple hours to find you but eventually Blue's hollers and howls guided us. When we got to you, you were covered in his dribble. He must have been licking you for days trying to wake you; he never left your side." I reach out and put my hand on Blue, who is still by my side.

"I've only been out for an hour or two though. I talked to you just yesterday. I was talking and then the others. . ."

"Lucas, I haven't heard from you for some time — it's been over a week now," Sam interrupts. "I knew something was wrong so I flew into Hawaii, rented a yacht, and sailed here to find you. It took a week just to get here. I was terrified we wouldn't get here in time. But we did," she smiles and wraps her sinewy arms around me.

"Sam, I talked to you a day or two ago," I insist. "I told you about the pictures I found and the people here."

"No, Lucas, you didn't. We last spoke when you were a day away from arriving to Palmyra Atoll. I just prayed that you made it here." Sam pauses for a moment with a concerned look, peering intensely at me and asks, "What others are you talking about? You said you were talking to the others?"

"The friends I made here on the island," I say. "I couldn't have been knocked out this whole time because I've been all over the island and even met people; Klara, and Edmund, and. . . I wonder where they are now. They're probably wondering about this boat. . ."

"Who?" she asks over me. "Lucas, we've been all over Palmyra searching for you and there was no one else on the island. It's just you."

"No, that can't be," I persist. "I know they packed their cabins up already, but they have to be somewhere. I swear, Sam, I told you about them already."

"Listen, Lucas," Sam says firmly, holding both my hands in hers. Her expression, body language and tone are just like the day my grandma told Leah and me about mom walking out on us. "There is no sign of life anywhere; and you and I haven't spoken about Palmyra at all. That is why I'm here now. When I didn't hear from you at our scheduled time I knew something was wrong. I got worried when my calls went unanswered for days. I sent a search plane out from Hawaii to see if Betsy was there, and she was. It was the only boat they could see. They couldn't land though; the disused runway hasn't been touched for decades. We last spoke the day before you were to arrive in Palmyra."

"This is a lot to take in," I say staring at my hands. They look so frail. I realize how thin they are, and my wrists. I jerk my hands to my stomach and feel. I must be twenty pounds lighter than I was!

"But there's more," Sam says as my hands explore my gaunt figure. "I really started getting worried when I learned about the history of Palmyra."

"What history?"

"I asked one of the professors at California Maritime Museum about the island, just because I didn't know much about it. When he called me back and told me its history, I immediately knew that something would happen. I could just feel it."

"What was it. . . that the professor said, I mean. What was so spooky you got a bad vibe and came out here?"

"So this is going to sound superstitious, I know, but I swear, Lucas, there is something going on on this island; something... supernatural."

"That does sound superstitious," I joke as my lips curl into a grin. The skin busts open on the top lip and I taste my own blood; it tastes like warm copper on my tongue. Sam grabs a tissue and hands it to me and then goes on.

"I know, but hear me out here. Palmyra has a haunting past—I mean really haunting. One unexplained thing after another has happened out here, and it has been happening for ages. People think the place is cursed, Lucas. And you know, I think I do too."

"Well, tell me what you found out then," I urge.

"Okay, let me see. Well, first of all, it was only discovered by accident when the captain of a ship went to bed one night and woke up three times with a terrible feeling —a premonition an article I read called it. He had his helmsman lay the ship to rest for the night and the next morning when they woke up they all saw that they were headed straight for a giant section of coral reef that would've sunk the ship. This was in 1798, so they didn't have all the technology we do now to warn them."

"I knew that," I say, and an uneasy feeling grabs hold of me. "I've heard that story, I swear. Edmund told me that."

The color suddenly drains from Sam's face and a hand darts to her lips. "Who did you say told you that?"

"Edmund," I repeat. "I mentioned him earlier. The one you claim isn't here."

"The captain's name was Edmund, Lucas. Edmund, something with an *F* I think."

"Fanning?" I say, and I feel the blood slip from my own face as well.

"That's it! Edmund Fanning. He was the captain of the ship; he found Palmyra by accident when he almost wrecked into it. Did you say you *met* Edmund Fanning? Because that is impossible. He's been dead for almost two centuries."

"Never mind that. Go on," I say, trying to wrap my brain around what all this means.

"Okay. Well that is something we need to discuss, Lucas. If you were talking to dead people then..."

"Please just tell me the rest, Sam," I snap, more brusque than I intended to come off.

"You don't have to be so curt, Lucas. I'm just trying to understand."

"Look, I'm sorry. So am I. I just need to hear the rest so I can—so *we* can understand."

"Okay," Sam says, and I know her tone. I've hurt her feelings. I feel a twinge of remorse for my outburst, but more than that I feel as if I've seen, no met, a ghost. "So anyway, even though this Edmund found the island, it wasn't until the early 1800's, like 1802 if I remember right, that this other captain came along and he did hit the reef. He was shipwrecked with his crew and that is where the island got its name. His boat was the Palmyra. I can't for the life of me think of his name now..."

"Sawle," I whisper.

"What?"

"His name was Captain Sawle, and I also knew that story."

"Lucas this is getting really weird," Sam says as she wraps herself up in a bear hug, as if to protect her soul from something.

"There was a man I met... or dreamt, or whatever. His name was Captain Sawle. I saw a bell by his shack that had that date, 1802, on it. He kept scrolls, scrolls that were about me I think, and..."

"I think it's good I found you, Lucas."

"None of the people were bad though, Sam. They all taught me so much."

"Well there weren't just captains that came here."

"What do you mean?"

"Those were the more innocent of the stories," she shivers. "There is also supposedly gold buried there, Incan gold, that was hidden by pirates who were shipwrecked."

"That doesn't seem too ghastly."

"Maybe that doesn't, but there was also a mysterious double murder, and that was only in the seventies. A wealthy couple sailed out here and were killed by a convict who made his way to Palmyra with his girlfriend and took up residence. The man's body was never found. I actually have all the stuff printed out somewhere," she says getting up from the floor where we've been sitting. She walks over to one of the built-in cabinets and rifles around and pulls out a navy blue folder with something scribbled in Sharpie across it, "Here it is."

Flipping through the notebook and scanning the pages she mumbles off some other events.

"In 1855 a whaling boat was shipwrecked here and no one ever found the crew. It looks like it was also used during World War II."

"They told me all that. I just don't get how that couldn't have been real," I shake my head. "What about Wilkinson or Judd?" I ask.

"What about them?"

"Is there anything in there about anyone with either of those names?"

Sam continues to scour through all the papers in the folder. Her eyes zigzag across the pages like the scroll of a typewriter moving along a piece of typing paper.

"Nothing in this piece written about the curses, but I have some other stuff." She continues to search and then her eyes stop. "Oh my gosh, Lucas!" she exclaims, her finger pounding down on the paper before her. "Gerrit Judd was a doctor from the US who claimed Palmyra in 1859. And there was a man named JB Wilkinson who owned the place after that in 1862, and his rights went to his widow when he died, Kalama was her name." She looks up at me. "How did you know that?"

"I met them all," I say. "I talked to them and ate with them and lived with them. It all felt so real..."

"You are not going to believe this," Sam sputters. "I just read here that Edmund Fanning's boat was also named Betsy! I am covered in goose bumps, Lucas. What in the world is going on?"

"I guess this is just an island of souls," I tell her. "And being unconscious I was able to meet them all."

"Does that not give you the creeps just a little?" Sam asks.

"No, actually, not at all."

"Why not?"

"Because this trip would have been nothing without them."

18

"Where are we going?" I ask Sam. "How long have I been out?"

"It's been a good four hours," she replies glancing at her watch, and then adds, "And we are on our way to Hawaii to get you medical care."

I dart up from the makeshift bed I am lying on and my brain goes fuzzy for a minute. I clench my eyes closed as a flame ignites inside me and ask, "What about Betsy?"

"We had to leave her on Palmyra. You can collect her when you're feeling better."

"You did what?"

"Listen, Lucas, we..."

"No, Sam. You know that won't work. You tell whoever to turn around for Betsy. I'm not just leaving her on Palmyra for God knows how long."

Sam and I have had our little spats through the years, but I have never been so frustrated with her as I am now. If anyone knows me, it is Sam. And she knows that Betsy is my everything. That she could just leave her out there without even consulting me is just...

It is the people we love who matter most in life, Lucas. I feel Klara with me suddenly, and the shaman, and even Edmund. I breathe in deep, refocus my energy, and exhale

the anger. I hear the shaman's words echoing in my soul:
*It is your heart and the vision you decide to see that guides your
future... What future will you create from this point forward?*

"Lucas, I know that your boat is your..."

"No, you're right," I stop her. "The boat will be fine.
It's a boat; it's just a boat. And it will be fine until I can
go back for her; besides it's insured."

Sam smiles softly and glances at me with a set of eyes
I've never seen her wear.

"What?" I ask, curious about this expression that is
completely foreign, to both of us.

"Nothing," she beams.

"You have a strange look on your face, Sam. You
look... different."

"Yeah, well, you *sound* different."

"I guess I do," I blush.

"So, anyway, Lucas, were you doing some writing on
the island?" Sam asks, and for some reason I feel relieved
at the change of subject.

"What do you mean?"

"I mean I found these and I just figured it was you,"
Sam says as she walks over to her bag and pulls out some
papers.

"We found these lying next to you. They look like
some sort of scrolls. I can't imagine where you even found
a scroll to write on, but it looks like your writing."

"Those look like the..." I grab the scrolls from Sam
and my eyes float over the words. I feel my face burn hot
as I mouth the words silently. I don't dare look up at Sam.

"I didn't mean to, but I had to take a peek. Look,
Lucas..."

"I'm sorry," I blurt. "You should've never seen this. I was probably delirious when I wrote this. It was part of my hallucination and I... Look, let's just forget about it because it..."

"Stop, Lucas," Sam demands. "Listen, I have to tell you something."

Sam's hazel eyes are as smooth and glassy as a reflection and they are locked-in on mine. I can't blink, can't look away from her no matter how much I want to, because in a way, I don't want to. This whole conversation feels like another dream. My body is weightless again and my head afloat in the stratosphere. I suck my breath in and wait.

"I need to tell you something right now, Lucas; something I've always wanted to say but have never had the courage to."

I can tell she is a little nervous as her voice quivers yet in someways I kind of like it, so I let her go on. I nod, my eyes still locked with hers. She takes a breath and continues. My stomach is in a wad and my palms are wet as I wait for her to talk again.

"I was waiting for you to tell me all these years the things I read in that scroll. I've waited and waited. I've almost gone crazy, and almost walked out on our friendship because I thought I couldn't handle it. But now that I know the truth, I have the courage to tell you."

"Sam... I..."

"Lucas, I have been in love with you for years. I have tried to tell myself I shouldn't be, tried to make you fall in love with me, and even tried to convince myself I wasn't, but I was; I am. Lucas, I love you, and not like a friend. I *love* you, love you."

"Sam, I..."

"I know you do," she smiles. "I read it," she says, tapping her finger on the scroll I am holding.

My stomach comes out of its tangle. The heat in my face dissipates and a new sensation consumes me. My thoughts swirl in a rose-colored fog. I put the scroll down and pull Sam to me. I lift her from the ground and hold her close to me, breathing her in—the smell of mango and salt from her skin. Her legs wrap around my waste as I hold her. The strength of her embrace matches mine. It feels like neither of us can get close enough.

"I love you," I whisper through her hair into her ear. "Thank you for never giving up on me, for never walking out."

I've hugged Sam a thousand times before, but she feels new in my arms. This feels new. I am completely out of my comfort zone, but okay. I drink in the moment. I am letting my guard down. I am creating my future right now, with Sam. Standing silently, locked in each other's embrace, I think I can physically feel our connection—a soul connection. Our love seems tangible for a moment.

We both finally loosen our grip and I set Sam back on her feet. She looks more beautiful than ever. She seems to glow as she stands in front of me. Of all the moments I have had since on Palmyra, this might be the most intense.

"So what do we do now then?" I ask.

"We'll figure it out," she says as she leans into me and presses her lips to mine. "We're both intelligent enough."

"I guess we will." I grab Sam's hands and hold them as we stand facing one another in the living quarters of the boat. Just as I'm about to say something, two of the rescue crew walk in. I drop Sam's hands and take a step back. We act like a couple caught having an affair. I chuckle under my breath at our newness to all this.

"Sorry if we interrupted," a tall, stringy man with long, thin muscles and permanently tanned skin says to us.

"No, you're fine," Sam insists. "What's up?"

"We were just going to grab a couple cups of coffee. We've got quite a trip ahead."

"Absolutely," she says, and the two of us step out of the way so they can pass to get to the kitchenette.

"Oh, I almost forgot," Sam turns to me again. "I also found these. They look like some old photos. Who are they?" she asks as she fans out a number of photos that she's pulled out of the file on Palmyra. They are the photos of Edmund and the others. I take them from Sam and study them.

"This is so strange," I murmur as I look through the faded snapshots.

"What is?"

"These are photos of everyone on the island — the people I was talking about. There's Klara smiling surrounded by butterflies in the field. And here's the Shaman," I say holding a photo of the weathered shaman out for Sam to see. "This is a rare one."

"What do you mean?" she asks.

"He was so serious, but here he's smiling near his hut. See all those things nearby?" I point to the animal skins and a totem. "Those are all from the Shasta tribal rituals. He was a shaman for the Shasta."

"But that was just a dream, Lucas. You didn't really meet anyone. These can't..."

"Oh, it was much more than that," I grin. "It may have all been in my mind, but it was much more than a dream. Whatever it was, it was real to me."

Sam is caught in a thought, perhaps pondering the idea. I return to the photos and next I see one of Captain Sawle standing near the Miracle Tree. He's holding a scroll in his hand and standing amongst his ship relics. There is also one of the Wilkinsons and Dr. Judd.

"These aren't the photos I saw back on the island," I mumble. "They were different. The ones I told you about…"

"You never told me about photos. Remember, we never spoke after you arrived?"

"Yes, right," I say. "I guess I mean they aren't the same ones I had seen earlier. They are…" I stop mid-sentence and notice something about the photos. I spread them across the small table in the saloon. I hunch forward and ease my face into the pictures as I scan my eyes from left to right. *Everyone is holding a scroll!* Every single shot, they are all holding scrolls, the same one I was just holding; the one that Sam read and handed to me.

"Are you okay, Lucas?"

"Yeah," I sigh. "I am actually. Better than ever I think to be honest."

"And you still aren't freaked out by all this?"

"I'm a little shaken, sure," I admit, "but not freaked out I don't think. It's something different I feel, but not freaked out… maybe humbled."

"Humbled?" Sam asks with searching eyes.

"Yeah, humbled."

"Why humbled?"

"Because this experience taught me so much, all of them did."

"What do you mean?"

"See Klara there? She's the one surrounded by butterflies. She taught me that beauty can only exist when there is harmony — and that peace exists within each one of us. We can let go of the struggle and let pain teach us; even suffering serves a purpose. If we want happiness, we have to find a way to balance out, even with outside forces working against us. She taught me how to really feel alive again."

"That's good advice," Sam replies.

"I know," I say and continue on. "And here are the Wilkinsons who showed me the significance of connection. And the Captain here, he showed me that the plants, the earth, this life — it keeps us nourished and healthy; and reminded me that it's this moment right now that truly matters not the past. Dr. Judd here," I say pointing to a picture of the doctor in his fishing gear, "showed me that light can illuminate the dark, when we acknowledge its strength and presence; and when we live from the heart we can trust the whispers of our guides to show us the right way. Then there's the shaman, who taught me that life has meaning and that we must stay true to our purpose. When we do, we have a sense of belonging, and walk in harmony with our soul's intention."

"That's pretty amazing," Sam says as she leans into me.

"It is," I nod and pull up a picture of Edmund. "And my buddy Edmund taught me so many awesome things, about having fun and that pleasure is an important part of life — a part I've been missing; and about trust — to trust and surrender to something greater than myself."

"And they all taught me about the importance of love and connection — to live from the heart and always acknowledge the light. There's no need to fight the darkness, sometimes we need a fog to settle over us to remind us of the light. And no matter what happens, I now know there is always light within the dark."

"Something really happened to your out there," Sam whispers to me, as if she finally believes me.

"Something did," I say still staring at all the photos that lay before me. "Whatever this is, I now know that the answers I came seeking from Palmyra — all those questions I thought were so pressing — don't need an answer at all. The treasure isn't found in the answers, but is hidden in the search; it's hidden in the act of seeking. We must never stop asking the questions and seeking their answers. By trusting our Creator, I will be guided to where I need to be. If I play my part, the universe will play its part."

"I'll be happy to accompany you," Sam grins. I lean down and kiss her.

"I couldn't imagine a better partner to take with me. Oh… and you too, of course, Blue," I say to my canine pal as he looks up at me, as though he understands.

I shovel all the photos on the table into my hand and straighten them by tapping them on my palm. I flip the photos as if they were the pages of a small book and then collapse on the small sofa. Sam snuggles in beside me, nuzzling into me like a kitten. I put an arm around her and think about everything that happened this past week, or however long I was in that cave back on Palmyra. I take a deep breath, kiss the crown of Sam's head, and close my eyes.

"Going to sleep?" Sam asks.

"Maybe just for a bit," I tell her. "To say goodbye to some friends."

ZZZZZ

"We're only a few hours away from Hawaii now," the captain calls into us and startles me.

"Thanks so much," I call back. One of the photos drops to the floor and Sam leans over to grab it.

"What's this?" she asks as she hands me the photo.

I take the worn matte paper in my hand and turn it over. On the back of the picture of Edmund a note is scribbled. I read what it says:

> *When all you see is darkness... turn to hope...*
> *and your heart will see the light.*
> *You never walk alone.*
> *We are always by your side.*

THE END.

Acknowledgements

Behind every great book is an incredible team—working their magic behind the scenes. This book could not have been written without their guidance, support and encouragement. First and foremost I must thank our Creator —for *everything*; my *Soul* family all over the world—this is for you! Much love, light, and gratitude for all your love and support; my family for their loving guidance and for always being there for me; and a massive thank you to my friend, editor, and literary maven, Cassandra W. Powers—you are truly amazing; and Teresa Kennedy and Danielle Forrest for their words of literary wisdom. And for anyone I may have missed... you know who you are... Thank You!!!

A Note from the Author

To hear about my latest books, sign up for my exclusive
New Release Mailing List and be the first to know:
www.Ljubincic.com/updates

I would love to know what you thought
of my novel! If you've enjoyed this book,
would you consider reviewing it on
www.Amazon.com and www.Goodreads.com?

CPSIA infor
Printed in th
LVOW04s1
451316

104